Contents

Chapter	1
1. Chapter One	2
2. Chapter Two	12
3. Chapter Three	22
4. Chapter Four	33
5. Chapter Five	45
6. Chapter Six	58
7. Chapter Seven	70
8. Chapter Eight	79
9. Chapter Nine	91
10. Chapter Ten	101
11. Chapter Eleven	111
12. Chapter Twelve	118
13. Chapter Thirteen	125
14. Chapter Fourteen	132
15. Chapter Fifteen	142

16. Chapter Sixteen   150
17. Chapter Seventeen   159
18. Chapter Eighteen   167
19. Chapter Nineteen   173
20. Chapter Twenty   179
21. Chapter Twenty-One   186
22. Chapter Twenty-Two   192
23. Chapter Twenty-Three   198

UNTOUCHED

Harry J. Miller

Copyright © 2022 by Harry J. Miller

All rights reserved.

No portion of this book may be reproduced in any form without written permission from the publisher or author, except as permitted by U.S. copyright law.

Ellen's attacker was killed in broad daylight under unusual circumstances. One minute he was behind her; the next, caught between the hoods of two cars. That's when she questioned how normal she truly was.

But when she becomes exposed to an unknown world, she quickly learns that there is more to life than meets the eye. Necromancers, sleight of hands, illusions, and trickery are amongst the many tools used by others to hunt her kind. The struggle becomes real as she fights to remain untouched; all whilst in the middle of an epic blood battle between good versus evil.

Chapter One

Her feet pounded the bitumen as she continued to run down the long, service alleyway. The backs of the tall, lifeless high-rise buildings passed her in a blur as she tried to pick up speed. Her hair, her clothes, were soaked from the downpour of cold rain which only added more weight to her body. If she could ditch them she would but this wasn't an option that was available to her. The sound of thunder grew louder as it growled overhead in the distance. The sudden storm that had blanketed the city was not going to disappear anytime soon.

She fought as panic threatened to take over her mind.

She clutched at her torso, her heart beating rapidly as if someone was playing it like a drum. She tried to take steady breaths but it was to no avail; sharp pain shot somewhere near her hips and she felt herself fall off her feet and onto the narrow road. The tiny stones dug their way into her skin and her hands automatically flew to her freshly grazed knee. The water stung and she cursed to herself.

Her stalker would well and truly catch her now. It was over.

Closing her eyes, sixteen year old Ellen raised her face towards the sliver of charcoal sky that was framed by the cold buildings that surrounded her. She felt each individual drop of rain fall onto her face and then trickle into her sodden blonde hair. Ellen omitted a barely audible sigh as she expelled a lungful of air. The pain was too much for her to push through; she wouldn't be able get back onto her feet in this form.

The voice whispering in her mind told her like it was, a straight-shooter as was she.

She was defeated.

For the first time in her life she found herself praying.

Who she was praying to, she didn't know. She hoped that someone - a higher, divine being - was listening to her desperate cries for help. She wanted to survive. She didn't want it to end this way.

She was young; she had her life ahead of her.

Opening her eyes, she looked up and down the alleyway searching for any signs of movement.

None. Not even the slightest twitch of a muscle.

She could hear the rain hitting the bitumen and the faint sound of city traffic coming from somewhere beyond the buildings. But there were no footsteps which she was so convinced that she would hear. The footsteps would have paralysed her with fear.

To this she was grateful.

Taking this as a good omen and feeling instant relief wash over her body, Ellen picked herself up onto her feet and limped ever-so-slowly down the narrow road in the opposite direction from which she came. The sound of cars grew more distinct with each step she took. The motor groans and grumbles were suddenly pierced with the wailing of emergency sirens - an ambulance perhaps?

The combination of rain, slick roads, cars, and human error was an accident just waiting to happen. It was as if the grim reaper was waiting in the darkness to claim yet another life to his growing number.

Another statistic in the accident and injury books and even more repairs that the city would have to pay for from crying tax payers coffers.

She turned the corner into yet another alleyway, this one narrower than the last, and she felt a smile break across her face. There was an opening at the end and she saw throngs of people huddled together. Her mind told her to push on, push through the pain that burdened her.

She could vanish into the crowd and no one would know she was there. She would become just another body making up the mass.

Most of all, she could be safe.

Breaking into a gander that was caught somewhere between a limp and a run, the newly identified safe haven began to loom in front of her. It seemed so close but yet, it remained so far. After what seemed like an eternity, she burst out from the mouth of the alleyway and into the bustling space where - by quick glance - at least two hundred people were gathered. They were pointing and gasping, excited about something which remained blocked out of Ellen's view. Feeling vulnerable, she jostled her way into the sea of people, taking care not to unintentionally elbow someone.

Handbags and umbrellas smacked her all over her body, and pointed corners pushed into her skin as if she was being tenderized for tonight's dinner. Rubbing the angry red patches that came to be on her forehead and arms, she emerged on the other side of the crowd.

Striped yellow-and-black barricades were placed in a makeshift ring to prevent onlookers from getting too close. But, like everyone knew, this didn't stop determined journalists from attempting to jump over them and grab a perfectly angled photograph. Attentive police officers, in the know of their tactics from experience, seized their arms and steered them back behind the barriers.

Do it again, they warned, and you will be taking photos from the inside of a police cruiser. Final warning buddy.

In this city, they were much like leeches. They were ruthless, ignorant, and had a blatant disregard for instructions if it meant that they got the best material out of all media outlets. Many of them had already cost innocent people's livelihoods and ruined countless reputations. This was all undeserved. It was only six months ago that a sorry excuse of a journalist was jailed for assaulting a child who had got in the way of unfolding news. The judges had bought the book down heavily on him for hitting the child with a camera.

Not only once.

Twice.

Several emergency vehicles - police, fire and paramedics - were parked strategically to try and block as much of the view from civilians as possible. The bodies of the vehicles guarded most of the scene, but not all of it. Their presence on site would explain the wailing sirens she heard earlier. These were now silenced although the flashing lights still danced in their clear plastic shells. Each officer on the scene seemed to take no notice of the rain as they were locked onto the situation at hand. They were not only great at their careers, but they were also passionate about their community.

Ellen shifted herself to the left by a few meters and then peered between the gap that was made by the bonnet of a cruiser and the back of emergency response paramedic SUV. There were two sedans, now fused together by what appeared to be a head-on collision. The airbags of each vehicle had deployed and from what she could see, the drivers had escaped or had been removed by the jaws-of-life. The hydraulic machine lay close by, having saved more lives. Oils were leaking from busted lines, colourful from reflecting the cloud-curtained sunlight.

She adjusted herself again slightly, eager to see more. She felt herself dry retching at the sight of what her eyes and mind were registering. There was someone jammed between the two cars that had collided, his body flayed in grotesque angles that were well outside of what a human, a contortionist even, was capable of achieving.

His face was frozen and portrayed no emotion, not even pain.

His forehead was battered, bruised and bleeding from where it had intercepted with the car. Other parts of his body were mutilated almost beyond recognition. The rain diluted and washed away the leaking blood into a nearby gutter.

Two police officers were now unraveling a black piece of plastic and holding it up as two others were preparing to fasten it to make a temporary screen. For those that had seen it, it was too little, too late. This scene would be burned into the back of their minds and their eyes for the rest of their lives.

No one seemed to take notice of Ellen as she began to hyperventilate and sway on her feet. She watched as the floor beneath her began to move, and as heat and clamminess douse her body. She turned on her heel and started to push her way through the gathered, ever-curious swarm of people.

She felt herself bump into those around her, earning several threatening glares. Eyes stared at her as she continued to clumsily fight her way out of the crowd. They were much like a school of fish, all huddled together and facing one direction. Reaching the edge of the school, she spied an empty bench underneath one of the only remaining natural rain-trees along this specific road.

It was within the heart of the southern shopping and business district; a playground for professionals, shoppers, recreationalists and people looking to have a coffee with friends or even alone to people gaze and watch the world carry on. Usually it was a handsome setting - towering, modern high-rises looking down onto a well landscaped and traffic-calmed road which was shared by vehicles and pedestrians alike. In the best of days, it offered an interesting balance of nature meeting the city.

But today, it was the polar opposite of handsome. It was in a state of tragedy and the storm cast more darkness.

Ellen reached the wooden bench and sat down, dropping her face into her palms and letting her fingers run through her wet hair.

Thoughts were speeding through her mind, none of them making any sense.

She recognised the man - indeed, he was the one that stalked, attacked and then gave chase to her. But why was he so adamant on catching her? She was but a sixteen year old girl with the same problems as everyone else had at that age.

She studied hard and put in nothing but the best effort at school. She always completed her homework on time and aspired to be a physiotherapist. A harmless physiotherapist so she could help people.

The biggest question she had was how did he go from being almost directly behind her to being pinned between two sedans?

Surely you had to have superhuman powers to be able to move that quickly. And everyone knew that superhumans were a fabrication of comic books; characters that were the figment of someone's imagination and put into ridiculous situations that were about as believable as the moon being made of cheddar cheese or a person coming back from the dead after being seriously maimed with countless witnesses.

She saw someone approach her from the corner of her eyes.

"Ma'am, are you alright?"

A young police officer walked around the bench and kneed down to be eye-level to her. He clapped both hands onto the knee which wasn't bent to the ground. His warm, hazel eyes met hers and she saw tufts of chocolate brown hair plastered against his forehead. Water drops fell from his navy blue hat and onto his shoulders.

"You seem a bit pale."

Lost for words, Ellen nodded. She knew she wouldn't be able to convince him no matter how hard she tried or how well she could act.

"Are your parents here? Friends?"

She shook her head.

"Would you like a lift home?"

She felt tears brim around her eyelids as the ordeal finally caught up with her. She didn't bother wiping these away as the rain was already doing this for her.

"Come on." The young officer stood up and helped her to her feet. Keeping a hand hovering behind her, he guided her to a cruiser that was parked on a side street but within close distance to the accident.

He opened the door for her and helped her in before closing it and getting in the other side. He turned off the crackling radio in the car which was used to coordinate the services to handle the situation they left behind. Using barely audible instructions whispered by Ellen, they pulled into her driveway slowly fifteen minutes later. The gravel crunched as the tyres drove over them and eventually, the cruiser came to a halt. Her parents were already standing at the door, a look of shock on their faces.

Was their baby girl arrested? Of course not! She wouldn't do such a thing although their neighbours were probably having a field day - something interesting happening in the sleepy neighbourhood at last.

Seeing the look of devastation on their daughters face as she left the car, they stepped to the side and let her disappear up the stairs and into her bedroom with no words being exchanged. A young officer emerged from the driver's side, took off his hat, and held it underneath his armpit. He spoke in an ashen voice, careful so that the traumatised girl upstairs couldn't hear them.

"There's been a terrible accident downtown today. She saw the scene and..." he began.

"We saw it on the news," her Dad replied. He was a well-built man but lean and towered over the officer. He had a tender arm around his wife who bared striking resemblance to her daughter. "What happened?" The three adults stood huddled underneath the façade of the large home as the storm persisted. More thunder rumbled and lightning struck the ground in the distance.

"We can't give full details as of yet but a pedestrian was caught between a two motor vehicle collision. He seemed to have appeared almost out of thin air according to one of the witnesses. It was very ...sudden. Quite eerie really. Given this weather though..."

Ellen's mother bowed her head at the thought of her daughter stumbling upon such a horrendous scene at her age.

As if reading her mind, the officer continued. "The city has services available for those that have experienced something so traumatic. I strongly urge you get in touch with any of the stations. They can provide you with any information you may be interested in." He placed his hat back onto his head and touched the brim of it.

"Sir. Ma'am."

He made his way back to his car but had the strong feeling that eyes were watching him. With a foot in the car, he turned around and peered up at a large, second-storey window that faced out onto the driveway. He saw the young girl staring down at him, her eyes wide open reminding him of an owl. He raised his hand in a small wave. She continued staring at him, unmoved by the small gesture.

A cold chill ran up his spine.

Something was quite eerie indeed.

Chapter Two

Ellen sat on her bed, her back and head propped up on the black wooden backboard. She clenched her fist into a tight ball before relaxing and letting it open. It reminded her of a flower coming into bloom. Although other's may find it laughable, it made her feel calm and at peace with the world.

Her room was dimly lit by a desk lamp angled towards the wall, and the cream walls had become more like a shade of grey from the storm clouds outside. Textbooks were piled precariously on a corner of her desk, and her wet clothes which she wore that day were now placed in a wicker basket by the door. This was her bedroom for as long as she could remember; the only difference throughout the years being that the solid, wooden cot was replaced with an equally solid double bed and a study desk had been added at the start of her schooling journey.

The police officer had left a short time earlier but not before he took the opportunity to gaze up at Ellen from behind his cruiser. There was the look of pity in his eyes; his eyes that softened to be almost doe-like when he saw her.

It was as if they tried to tell her that everything would be okay.

But this was ridiculous.

He didn't know about anything that was going on in her life and it really was none of his business to intrude on uninvited. He wouldn't understand anyway so what was it to him?

The officer then waved at her, dropped himself behind the wheel and drove back down the driveway. He turned the corner, kicking up loose gravel that got caught in the treads of the tyres as he went. As he disappeared, Ellen felt herself relax on the bed. Her body became light and her head slid down the headboard onto the soft, white pillow. A deep state of thoughtfulness threatened to take her mind hostage and it took mere seconds for it to be successful in that battle. Her brain kicked into overdrive and started shifting through her thoughts. No matter how hard she was pushing her mind - no matter how hard she was pushing herself to the edges of rationality - there were no realistic explanations available to account for what she had experienced and seen firsthand ever since she turned sixteen.

The first of these incidents happened on none other than the day after her sixteenth birthday. Her head was buried deep within biology books that were piled around her on a desk at the back of the library. Studiously, she jotted helpful notes which would prove to be useful in an upcoming exam for bonus credits later that week. The library was normally a peaceful place except for that day. Someone whom she recognised as being in the grade above her sat at a neighbouring table, and ripped his headphones out of the jack on his phone. Instantly, the music he listened to blared for everyone else to hear and it most certainly wasn't tasteful.

Ellen muttered to herself, and hoped that the librarian would throw him out. Ironically, the elderly woman was nowhere in sight and neither was her assistant.

"Excuse me, do you mind?" she called out to him with an air of irritation. He rocked back on his chair and flipped the bird before making the music, if you could call it that, louder.

Irritated, she slammed the heavy book shut with a loud thud! and cursed him in her sigh. Almost instantly, she heard a thunderous crash and looked back up.

One of the legs of the chair had snapped in half and splinters had flown all over the charcoal carpet. The ignorant boy was now on his side, red faced and with blood pouring from his crooked nose. His hands flew to his face and he began to wail like the little brat that he was. Ellen heard scuffling and the librarian had appeared with a handful of books. Her assistant – a fresh graduate from university – was hot on her heels and tried to stifle a giggle at the sight albeit, with great difficulty.

"What happened?" asked the librarian, pushing the stack of books onto the table. She had grey, flyaway hair and always wore a brown apron over subdued clothes. She had been with the library for decades and was constantly badgering people to be respectful of their surroundings and to use furniture as intended. She had become a staple to the place and it was suspected that she would stay here for the rest of her days.

"I honestly don't know. I asked him to be quiet, closed my book and he just... fell. The leg must have broken when he swung on it," Ellen replied. She was lost for words.

"Teenagers," muttered the elderly woman. Ellen assisted in putting everything away and left the library in a great hurry, the scene replaying in her mind as she went.

The second incident happened two weeks after the library accident. Ellen walked through the gates of the high school, making her way to the furthest block for math hour when she caught the sound of someone threatening another person. Looking around, she noticed Tom – a senior who happened to be a serial offender of school suspensions – towering over a weaker boy who was cowering away from him. Tom had a textbook in his hands and slammed it into the boy's chest upon seeing Ellen.

"Mark my words, git," he snarled into his ear. in the assertion of dominance, he pushed his shoulder into Ellen as he ambled past. "Move, you freak."

She ran up to the tormented teenager and convinced him to file a report with the principal. Nodding his head, he hitched his backpack onto his shoulders, whispered an appreciative thanks and scurried away. Ellen sincerely hoped that karma saw what had happened. To her surprise, this was answered by the end of the day.

In his aggression from being suspended, yet again, Tom had reversed a bit too quickly and crashed his roadster into the car behind him. An ambulance was called to treat a concussion he had received from hitting his forehead into the steering wheel, a result from his airbags failing to deploy. He was both the talk and butt of jokes for over a month, only ending when he decided to leave school and pursue vocational training instead.

He was his bosses problem now, no longer the care of the educational board.

Ellen continued mulling these thoughts but they became thinner and less comprehensive as her eyelids began to droop. She lost sense of time; time had let her go from its grasp. She succumbed to a deep slumber that welcomed her with open arms. Somewhere in the distance, she heard a musical voice call out to her. Hands wrapped themselves around her shoulder and guided her into an unknown abyss.

She now found herself in a handsome, wooden-paneled living room. There were two large, comfortable looking high-backed armchairs complimented by an antique wooden coffee table. The room was dimly lit by a roaring and delightful crackling fire in the fireplace which cast a warm hue across the room. The light twinkled off many crystals, glasses, and forged metal trinkets that lined the mantle and adjoining display cabinet. She walked forward cautiously, the rug beneath her feet feeling plush, and examined the intricately carved details of a trinket that was closest to her. It appeared to be a small figure of a man crouching in front of a rearing horse.

It was so quiet that she could hear herself breathing.

She moved to the next one; this one a forged goblet covered in odd symbols that were unfamiliar. It piqued her interest. Lifting a finger to get a better loo -

"I would not touch that if I was you. It doesn't belong to you."

The same, musical voice that called her name.

Ellen spun on her heel, lost balance and grabbed the edge of the mantle to steady herself. Her heart was racing in fright. She was so immersed at looking and admiring these figures that she forgot about her surroundings and had let herself be caught off-guard. It took her just over a minute for her eyes to adjust to the darkness and realise where the voice originated from.

In the doorway of the room, she was able to just make out two pinpricks – eyes – that reflected the dancing flames. They disappeared and reappeared in an instant.

The figure had blinked.

Frightened, Ellen stood rigidly still. This was like a scene from a horror movie. Unfortunately for her, she was no part of it.

The figure presumably took a step towards her because more of it – him – became visible. Long, metallic-silver hair grew from his scalp and fell mid-way down his back. His eyes, although difficult to make out, appeared to be a cold, steel-blue almost grey. His face was long and pointed; his cheeks angled, and nose chiseled and pointed. He had a pale complexion, almost translucent.

The stranger held a glass in his hand which looked to be filled with bronze spirits. Whiskey? She didn't know. The glass looked haunting though as it glinted from the fire. A black, shimmering robe hung from his slender, tall frame and pooled around him on the floor.

"A drink?" he offered, extending his hand towards the table between the armchairs. Ellen stared at disbelief. A silver tray had appeared, complete with a tumbler and several decanters containing liquids of different colours. She stared at disbelief – had this been here earlier or was she oblivious to it being there all along?

"No thank-you," she declined. "I'm not even of age to be drinking." Her voice was but a stammer from the fear that struck her heart.

What appeared to be laughter lines formed at the man's eyes and he let out a chuckle. But as quickly as it happened, he regained his mysterious composure.

"Well, at least sit down then."

Ellen did as she was instructed and took the armchair closest to the fire. It was more comfortable than she had expected. He sat on the arm of the other chair and gazed down his pointed nose at her. His voice returned to its musical and gentle state. "You are of age, Ellen."

"I'm sixteen," she argued. "That's not –."

He held a finger up to stop her, amusement dancing across his eyes.

"Tell me," he paused. One of his eyebrows shifted upwards. "Have things been happening that you can't explain? You wish for something to happen, and it does? Almost like magic?"

"There is no such thing as magic."

"Correct. We don't do magic. That's child's play but it's a stretch to say that it doesn't exist."

He clasped his hands together. Ellen had the faint impression that he was waiting for her to say something.

The man lamented on the fact that she seemed too stunned to say anything. By this stage, other gifted teenagers would have laughed and thought this was a joke; an entire figment of their dreams. They had a bit of a rebellious irk to them. Made it more entertaining but difficult to handle in the long run. Those that were frightened beyond their wits were returned back into a submissive dream-like state and then woken as if remembering an unrelated nightmare.

Only.

Ellen was taking it quite well. She was self-controlled and cautious. He knew those types too. She would listen and decide if this was real or just a dream later on. When he was certain she wasn't going to say anything, he progressed onwards. Now for the real test, the part that most found hardest to handle. He watched as her face remained composed and waiting.

"When you turn ten years old, you undergo monitoring by one of our kind." He elaborated on the our. It was important to distinguish the difference.

"If you portray desirable characteristics such as logic and wisdom, strength and loyalty, you get marked and acquire – get bestowed upon, for the want of a better term - a certain set of skills on your sixteenth birthday. It's much like coming of age. Generally people can't draw the linkages together between what happens on the ground and physical possibility of it happening but you were quick to put the pieces together. I commend you for that."

Ellen had a look of confusion on her face. She was still trying to put these pieces together however, it was difficult because it didn't make much sense. She rubbed her temples, trying to let everything sink in.

"I thought these sorts of things were handed down through families? You know, like bloodlines? At least, that's what books I've read were like..." she began.

"But this isn't a fiction book." His answer was so simple, so blunt and unsatisfying that disappointment welled inside her. Ellen slouched into the back of the chair.

"Those abilities that we give you are very real. With the proper training and education, they can affect everything and everyone around you and change their life paths." He spoke the last sentence as if it was a warning not to be taken lightly. "You can influence and alter the near future but it does come with a burden – you can't change the past."

He stood up on his feet and put his glass on the table.

"It's getting late. I trust we will be seeing each other again in the near future." He made his way to the doorway and looked back at Ellen, his robe trailing behind him. "For the time being, please be careful with what you wish for until you learn to control yourself. Good night."

She blinked once but he had already disappeared into the darkness.

Ellen stirred in her bed, opening her eyes. She let them adjust to the bright morning light that was filtering through her window and came to realise that she had fallen asleep in the clothes that she wore the previous afternoon. There was a faint buzzing coming from outside. Someone was mowing their lawn on this fresh Sunday morning.

She lingered in her bed for a while longer, staring at the blank ceiling and struggled to remember the details of the dream that she had the previous evening. It was an interesting one; a man had told her that she had been given powers that could let her control the world around her. She mused about this for a while longer before pulling herself out from beneath the blankets and planting her feet firmly on the carpet.

"My name is Ellen," she told herself. "And I am an ordinary sixteen year old girl."

Making her way to her dresser, she pulled out a casual t-shirt and shorts that she only ever wore around the house. They weren't the dressy, well-maintained type that she wore in public and she wasn't planning on doing anything outside of the four walls.

With these in hand, she started for the door but stepped on something small and sharp. Tears welled in her eyes, and she dropped the clothes onto her desk to free her hands so she could massage her foot. Her left hand clumsily brushed against the stack of books and they scattered all over the floor around her. There was a small, grey metal object laying there which was the perpetrator of the throbbing foot.

Cursing, she bent down and picked it up. The metal cold was cold against her fingertips.

It was a trinket; a man crouching under a rearing horse.

Last night's dream instantly rushed back to her. It really did happen. Ellen let out a deep sigh as all the questions and feeling of puzzlement reawakened within her like wildfire. It plunged her back into a feeling of limbo and despair.

"Maybe I'm not so ordinary after all."

Chapter Three

Ellen let out a content sigh as she slid through the door and back into her bedroom. Her pants were tight around her waist, the edges threatening to leave imprints on her skin if she didn't take them off in good time. Her mother was an amazing cook, this time whipping up the family favourite – beef stroganoff – and Ellen did not hesitate to tuck in. Family dinners were never large affairs but they did spark good conversations, this time revolving on the existence of life outside beyond Earth. Reaching the end of her philosophical wits, she helped clear the table and then made her way upstairs to her bedroom. The events from yesterday had fallen at the wayside and there, she hoped, it would stay. Uncomfortable, she wriggled out of the now too-tight pants and into her elasticized pyjamas.

Energised from the food and on a high from the euphoria of a productive day, she slipped into her chair behind the desk and pulled her laptop towards herself. There was enough time left in the evening to establish a solid heading on her English assignment although she knew that this wasn't due for a while.

Four weeks, to be exact.

She had also read Romeo and Juliet several times meaning that the she knew the ins-and-outs of it quite intimately and wouldn't need to spend time revising the playbook. This was all the better.

Grabbing a pen and a notepad from the top draw of her desk, she set about outlining an essay structure from the main words of the essay question. She took a moment to pause and glance up at the trinket that she had stepped on. This was now placed next to her desk lamp in the furthest-left corner of her desk, and the light gave it a twinkling glow.

Seeing it brought back a flood of memories from the previous evening; the dream that had actually turned out to be real. Or at least, planted into her mind through powers that she couldn't explain.

Was that possible? she thought. Was that within the range of the so-called skillset the silver-haired man spoke about?

Ellen drifted into a deep thought, the end of her pen automatically flying to her mouth so that it was now lodged between her teeth. It was a nasty habit. Her dentist told her so. But her visitor had left so many questions unanswered that she considered it to be acceptable just for this time.

Instinctively, she drew the laptop even closer to herself to the point that she was now hunched over the keyboard with a crooked back. Her mind was back in hyper drive. There was no attention spared to the assignment that was now pushed away and lay discarded on the side. Her hand was on her mouse, darting this way and that. With a few quick strokes of the wrist, she had a new browser tab open. She sat about identifying prime key words. Her fingers skimmed across the keyboard, hitting keys as they went.

Supernatural.

Ellen clicked the magnifying button on the right of the page. It turned white before presenting her with thousands of results. She skimmed over these as most were fan-sites of a popular supernatural television show which was a hot topic amongst her friends. Uninterested, she pondered for a brief minute before refining her search terms.

Supernatural AND humans.

Another pause as the web trawled through millions of sites and did the searching for her. It returned fewer results which she was thankful for, and the pages - at a glimpse - seemed much more in tune to what she was after. She clicked on the first link but was quick to discover that this described a higher deity – God – as being supernatural and the creator of all. Frustration began to rise inside her. This wasn't what she was searching for.

She bit her tongue, quickly jotting down the used search terms onto the paper in scrawled writing. Slipping the pen between her lips, trying yet another combination of keywords.

Supernatural AND humans AND history AND predictions.

Ellen, in hope, crossed her fingers underneath her desk and rocked back and forward as her request made its way around the world. Anxious, she uncrossed her fingers and drummed on the desk top. She hadn't realised that her heart had decided to skip faster.

"Third times the charm", she whispered to herself.

Again, results filled the screen, these looking more promising than the last. She clicked the first one after reading a vague description about recounts from past paranormal experiences. A black background blanketed the page, followed by white text about the origin of the website, photographs of supposedly supernatural beings and links to subpages. Scanning the menu, she found a page that was dedicated to different supernatural races. There were about a dozen listed but only one caught her eye – Tempusmantia. Drawn to it, she clicked. This led her to another page with the same black background and white text as the others. This particular page had no photos, just paragraphs. Although there were no visual aids, it could still be helpful in her quest for answers.

The Tempusmantia... she read, ...is one of the oldest recorded races deemed to be 'paranormal' and is the base of certain modern beliefs in which you are able to control your own destiny, and that your actions control flow-on effects in the future. The term 'Tempusmantia' translates roughly to "time divination". It is also commonly referred to as 'Tempusmancer' or 'Tempusmancy'.

Although not broadly known by paranormalists and enthusiasts, Dr R. Hiddlestone conducted significant research on this specific race. His work can be found in The Illusion of Time: The Fabrication of Fate. He noted that Tempusmancers are capable of bending time to suit their agendas but also possess a much greater range of powers such as dictating fate for themselves and others around them and to some extent, mind control. The extent of their powers remains unknown however, it is believed that they are able to practice divinations of other types. Tempusmancers are human-like in appearance with no obvious markings to distinguish them from ordinary humans. Their imprint on the human world is unable to be determined.

In the supernatural realm, Tempusmancers are thought to have one only one opposing race – Necromancers. Necromancers are known to practice communications with the departed, and believe that Tempusmancers obstruct this practice. They are also only capable of practicing this one divination type (see 'Necromancer'). This conflict has been the sole cause of several large 'wars' between the two factions. Other notable supernaturalists have been led to believe, throughout their research, that modern Necromancers are seeking the cleansing of all Tempusmancers however, this is yet to be proven and should be regarded as a myth for the time being.

A sense of disappointment blossomed within Ellen as she realised that she had finished reading the last of the the text on the page in front of her. Increasingly frustrated that there was no more information on the site, she wrote down the name of the book by Hiddlestone and made a mental promise to stop by the library on the way home from school the next day. She was aware that there was a small section dedicated to the paranormal and supernatural but didn't like her luck about this particular book seeing as it was published well over fifty years ago and the topic wasn't overly popular. She entered Tempusmancer into the search bar but all the search results were just rehashes of the information that she had already read. Taking this as a sign to complete her foray into the paranormal world for the evening, she closed this window and pulled her assignment back in front of her. Despite this gesture, she couldn't refocus her mind onto this menial task and turned the laptop off for the evening.

The ill-fated affair between Romeo and Juliet would have to wait until her brain was functional again.

Ellen rose from her chair, her eyes drooping and her bottom feeling numb from sitting. She glanced at the alarm clock that sat on her bedside table, sleepiness slowly taking her into its arms. The clocks large, ghastly luminous green numbers stared back, informing her that it was almost midnight. Astounded that time had escaped her as quickly as a hound in flight, she slipped between the light, soft sheets of her bed and turned off the lights. Darkness washed over the room, the blackness feeling oddly comforting and soothing to her eyes. She gave in to the temptation of sleep almost instantly, the occasional haunting hoot from of an owl outside of her window accompanying her until she closed her eyes for the final time that evening.

- - -

A nasally, loud buzzing came from somewhere deep within the grey-concrete administration building of Charles Hill High School. Doors from classrooms erupted open and students poured in to the well-kept, forested grounds. Ellen gathered her belongings rather slowly, packing her textbooks, pencil case, and notebooks into her bag. She preferred not to be trampled by the usual herd of students eager to leave for the day. The ferocity of some of them could be compared akin to wild animals. Zipping the now laden bag, she slung it over one of her shoulders and started towards the door.

"Ellen, can I talk to you before you go?"

Ellen paused in mid-step and turned to face her teacher. She could already feel the bag cut into her shoulder so she placed this at her feet.

"Is there something wrong?" she asked.

Mr James was a tall, muscular, middle-aged man with black hair and glasses perched on his nose. He was a favourite and much-loved teacher for his inclusive teaching practices and his ability to instil determination into even the hardest and most difficult students. Unknowingly, he was also the crush of many of his female students who took his classes just because of him. He primarily taught sciences but was knowledgeable about a broad range of topics, his personal favourite being astrophysics. He paced around his desk and sat on it with his legs dangling backwards and forwards, gazing at Ellen through his glasses. He was wearing a fitted black tshirt and black slacks with a silver belt. There was a twinkle in his eyes, and a warm smile on his face.

"Top marks again in last weeks test, Miss Nightingale. I wanted to ask where you see yourself after your senior year? That's coming up quite quickly so it's high time for you to make plans for what comes after." He clasped his hands in his lap.

"I am looking at going to university, sir. Physiotherapy hopefully," she replied, the tone of hope in her voice. This is what she had dreamed for ever since she was a child. "That's, if I get good enough grades and my application satisfies the university board."

"If you are getting top marks in other classes outside of mine, you have nothing to worry about. Have you considered the advanced streams of the sciences? I imagine you'd do well."

"I have and will be placing an application for it once intake has opened."

"Good. That's what I was hoping to hear. I just want to make sure you are on the right path." With that, he smiled with that same twinkle in his eyes, leaped off the desk and busied himself with putting away his own belongings.

Ellen picked up her bag again and hurried out the door, down the pathway to where her bicycle was locked up to a chain-link fence. A wide smile was stretching across her face. Knowing she was on the right track to success made her feel ever better.

It was a quick ride to the city library – Library of Charlemagne – approximately five minutes down a historic laneway lined with gorgeous dated buildings made of sandy-coloured stone. The large, rounded columns and intricate details were reminiscent of the both roman and gothic styles and added charm to the neighbourhood. Ellen enjoyed the breeze whipping through her hair as she pedalled down the cobbled way. Another historic building stood on the corner of the laneway where it intersected with a busy avenue. It was by far the largest and majestically dwarfed all others. Magnificent stained-glass windows stretched high into the sky and were shielded by deep eaves. A tall colonnade stretched around the outside of the building, with the middle two columns framing the entrance to the library. This was signified by two, heavy wooden doors that were opened and closed each day.

Chaining her bike up to a nearby rack, she walked through the doors and took a moment to marvel at the glorious interior. It was a massive, cavernous room complimented by high ceilings. Colours from the stained-glass windows projected downwards over the furniture, displaying a wide spectrum of colours like a rainbow. Comfortable, leather armchairs and beanbags were placed in small clusters around the room. There were two stories in this building. The ground floor was dedicated to fictional works and had rows of computers sitting on handsome, wooden desks made available to the public. Book cases sprawled in each direction, those lining the walls reaching to the roof. The first floor was home to non-fictional works and contained some of the oldest books within the region. These were generally only available on request though, in an effort to preserve them for generations to come.

When she finished her awing, Ellen climbed a staircase in the middle of the room to reach the top floor. Her fingers slid smoothly along the gold plating on the handrail. Having memorised each of the major sections on this floor, she had little difficulty in finding the 'paranormal' category. She ran her hand along the spines of the books as she searched, dust accumulating on her palm and individual particles drifting in the air around her. These books mustn't have been looked at for a long period of time. She spied a black, leather bound book with peeling gold lettering - Hiddlestone emblazed sidewards - and removed this from the line. She blew the dust off the corners and relief surged over her like a giant wave. It was exactly what she was seeking. Storing this under her arm, she made her way back downstairs and completed the checkout on a self-serve machine the library had recently installed as part of a customer service upgrade.

This piece of technology was a sharp contrast against the age of the building itself and she couldn't help but chuckle.

With the book now safely stowed in her bag, she kicked off from the curb and powered homewards, humming as she went. The mechanical noise of each pedal stroke never sounded so beautiful to her ears as it did now.

- - -

Ellen ripped the old book from her bag and placed it on her desk. She flicked the switch on her desk lamp and the gold lettering came to life, sparkling in the light. Excited and heart pumping, she ran her hand over the cover and opened it. A forward had been penned by Hiddlestone in the form of an introduction, followed by a comprehensive contents page. She turned another page, and a black and white aged photograph stared back at her. She pulled the lamp closer so it illuminated the page even more, giving her a clearer view. It was a group portrait with thirty faces glaring up at her. The group was standing in three lines, apart from the man in the middle of the first line. He was sitting in a throne-like chair and had the most regal face of all. Although not a coloured photograph, Ellen knew that this man's hair was metallic silver and his eyes were a cold, steel blue. It was the man that had visited her in her dreams two nights ago.

She gasped, the gasp piercing the sheer silence of her bedroom. Everything was piecing together just like the pieces of a puzzle. And then she was enveloped in silence, once again; the ticking of the grandfather clock downstairs the only thing that could be heard throughout house.

Tick.

Tock.

Chapter Four

Ellen ran a finger down the glossy page, continuing to look at the figures in the group photograph that stared back at her. She let her eyes wonder along the lines, quickly realizing that they were all men. She paused on one of the gentlemen in the third row, closest to the right; his lifeless eyes piercing into hers.

Those eyes. They seemed vaguely familiar!

Ellen struggled to come to grips with where she had seen them previously, and bit her lip. She knew she would remember eventually; she usually did. But nothing irked her more than seeing something that she had come across before and not being able to place it. She struggled for a brief moment more, the throbbing of her heart filling the daunting, silent void around her. Drawing blanks, she resigned the thought and stowed it in the back of mind. With a single finger, she snagged the corner of the page and turned it to the next one. It was a solid page of text, the word History blazoned across the top in bold, black wording. Assuming her normal study position – her head propped up by her hands with elbows on the desk – she began to immerse herself, the words dragging her into the story that was purposefully penned to be told. She was so consumed within the book that she hadn't realised that there was now a figure sitting on her bed, gazing; waiting. His arms were folded and his face neutral as if it was set into stone.

"There is only so much," he said softly, drawing out each word as they came out from his mouth. The words were almost filled with disdain. "That you should believe when reading books." His words sliced through the silence like a knife.

Ellen leaped out of her chair in fright, the trance that held her to the book now broken. She pushed herself up hard against the wall and noticed that the book was pushed onto the floor in her haste. It was now sprawled open to the page with the group photograph. It took every ounce of self-control to not let out a scream from the fright that riddled her body. The man that occupied the throne in the image, the man that had visited her previously, was now sitting on her bed with his eyes taking in Ellen's state. The light from the desk lamp distorted his features, making him look more foreboding than he actually was. Deep, dark shadows stretched across his face and the entertained smile on his face seemed sinister. He had changed clothes, and was no longer donning a long robe. Rather, he was impeccably dressed in a burgundy turtle-neck, three-quarter sleeve shirt and black, long cargo pants. These were complimented by a pair of highly shined black boots.

"Hello," he mused. "It's quite alarming how much humans can disengage themselves from reality when they are gripped by something.

It makes it easy to attack them from behind without them knowing that you're there."

He flashed his pearly white, perfect teeth at Ellen and picked himself off her bed. his body weight leaving a neat groove in the blankets. The man moved with grace, light on his feet, across the room and pulled the chair away from the desk. He knelt down and retrieved the book, closing the cover to analyse the front of it. His eyes glazed over as he scanned the aged, peeling-gold title. The words glinted eerily at Ellen. Ellen was still pushed up against the wall, a hand over her heart, trying to regain her elusive breath.

The man furrowed his brows.

"Ah," he sighed. "I'm all too familiar with Hiddlestone's work. He was a prime researcher back in the day but his integrity took a hit and he became lacking. By the time he had finished this particular book, he had entwined so many old wives' myths into it that it can hardly be described as being accurate. Quite frankly, this isn't even worth the paper it's written on nor the glue that holds it together."

He gazed up at Ellen, lifting one of his arms, and motioned for her to sit back down onto the chair which he had now positioned back at the desk. Ellen pushed herself off the wall and complied. He slid the book back onto the desk, open at the page with the photograph, and stood behind her. He reached over her left shoulder, pointing at the picture, and began speaking; his gentle voice carrying her into another world.

- - -

A young boy, no more than thirteen years of age, skipped down a dirt street, kicking his heels together and whistling as he went. Small puffs of dust lashed upwards with every step. The child's cheeks were cherub-like and hinted red; his eyes were still a baby blue. His grey cap was drawn down over his face but strands of blonde-silver hair peeked out from underneath. A large smile was spread across his face and his book-bag bounced jauntily against him as he made his way home from school. His mother often permitted him to stop by Elder Smith's workshop and it was here where he was heading to now. Elder Smith's wooden-boarded workshop was located centrally along the busy main-way which was often full with horses and carriages, and today was no exception. Seeing the workshop on the other side of the road, the young boy eyed distances between each carriage and made a dash for it. He was aware not to do risky runs across. His parents were honourable members of the community and they would find out quicker than he would arrive home. And this would most certainly come with punishment.

With over-brimming happiness, he crossed through the open doorway and into the warm cabin that acted as the shop area. The child caught orange-yellow anvil sparks from the corner of his eye and found Elder Smith hammering a heated piece of metal, forging something he didn't recognise.

"Eldy Smith!" he proclaimed in a not-yet-matured voice.

The blacksmith looked up at the child, sweat pouring down his face. He was a very stoutly man, and short; his brown shirt and black crafting apron were filthy, as were his hands. His sandy hair was covered in grime. His tight lips stretched upwards as he gave the newcomer a toothy grin.

"Aye, Master Grey. What would your parents say if they knew the way you were speaking?" he poked, with a brogue. The hammer he was holding was placed onto a workbench and he waddled to the boy. He sat down on a stool and took the boy onto his lap.

"I'm sorry. Whatever you do, please don't tell them!" Hans Grey begged. He didn't want to be punished!

"You know I'm just fooling around," the blacksmith laughed. "What can I do for you today?"

"A story?" the boy asked, hopeful. The blacksmith always told the best stories! The blacksmith opened his mouth but another man had appeared in the doorway dressed in travelling robes. He was clean and well-dressed, the opposite of the blacksmith.

"Master Melvin," the blacksmith acknowledged, and gently took Hans from his lap and stood him on the ground.

"Good afternoon Artisan Smith. I presume you've finished my request?" the other man asked. He was tall and severe looking with black hair and dark brown eyes. He peered at Hans through those dark eyes and then back at the blacksmith.

"Of course!" Smith rushed to the back of the workshop and retrieved a large, long object that was sheaved in silk. He bowed deeply as he passed it across. "To your dimensions, sir."

The man took the object and gave the blacksmith a pouch which rattled every time it moved. Gold. "Payment to where it is due for your constant, fine workmanship." He turned back to Hans and knelt down so he was now eye level with him. The silk-sheaved package protruded away from him. Matured eyes now stared into youthful ones.

"I trust the young master has been keeping out of trouble?" he asked. Hans took a step backward, surprised and wide-eyed, looking at his blacksmith friend for encouragement.

"Go on son, he's a friend to your parents," Smith urged.

"Yes, sir," the boy replied politely.

The man kept eye contact with the child, smiled, and placed his empty hand on Hans' shoulders. He gave it a tight squeeze and Hans immediately felt warmth spread throughout his body like his blood was being boiled. It passed as quickly as it came.

Standing back onto his feet, the man nodded curtly to the blacksmith and hurried out of the workshop into the busy street.

"What did you make him, Eldy Smith?" asked Hans, curiously.

"Oh, that's between me and him. Now shouldn't you be running home, young master? I expect your parents would have dinner ready and you still need a wash." The stoutly blacksmith gave the same, toothy grin and watched on, hands on his hips, as the boy carried himself home.

Hans kicked at the dirt, watching fragments of rocks forcefully fly away. His head was hanged and he muttered random, incoherent sentences quietly to himself. But this didn't last long. As he rounded the final corner to his home, he saw the two storey manor engulfed in flames. Well-meaning community members surrounded it, attempting to extinguish it with buckets of water. Others were crowded around the burning home, screaming and looking for ways to help. Thick, black plumes of smoke polluted the air around them making it hard to breathe, like you were trying to suck oxygen out of water.

Grey snow fell from the heavens and onto his cheek. Only, it wasn't snow but rather ash from his home. Tears welled under his eyes and he felt them roll down, making clear, meandering channels through the fallen ash. Sadness shot through his heart and it seemed that his life had stopped and was now standing still. He felt a hand drop onto his shoulder and the man from Eldy Smith's shop looked down at him sombrely. They both looked at each other for an indefinite amount of time, trying to find comfort in each other. No matter how hard the child looked, comfort was not something to be found.

Deep down inside, Hans knew that he had just become an orphan.

It was a rainy day when Master Melvin called a sixteen-year old Hans into his large, wooden-panelled stateroom and had told him that he was different. He was, what they called, a Tempusmancer; a figure that had the ability to control time and fate, and he had bestowed this gift on Hans in the blacksmith workshop when he was thirteen. Why? Hans asked.

Because I had a premonition that tragedy would strike that evening, was the reply. And indeed it had, with a fire being the tragic conclusion to his parents' lives.

The conversation was surreal to Hans, and was deep and emotional.

During this time, he had come to learn that Melvin had an estranged brother that had turned his back on the family and was never heard of again; that was, until Melvin had undertaken his own training and became a Master. The Masters were part of the Grand Committee and had the responsibility to determine the future of the race as well as investigate any phenomenons that involved them. There came a time when the Masters had to investigate the disappearance of several Tempusmancers, some of whose dismembered bodies were found across the globe. It was concluded that a different race, Necromancers, had begun a purge so they could use their DNA and blood samples to develop a hybrid of races. To Melvin's chagrin, it was led by none other than his brother. Where he was hiding and controlling his pawns from remained unknown. Necromancers were only able to converse with the dead and their powers to learn other divinations were rather limited to that of their counterparts.

As the years passed, Hans became more refined at his craft, spending countless hours taking notes from his teacher's lessons. Although his acquired skills seemed great, they came with great responsibility and this he kept at the back of his ever-ticking mind.

Be careful where you tread because you could be upsetting a delicate balance.

He could determine peoples fate, bend time to make it seem like there was more of it, and influence those around him to a high degree. Over a dinner, he had asked why Melvin couldn't change the fate of his parents. To this, he explained to Hans that there were things you can't change no matter how hard you try. He didn't say more.

Tragedy struck once again on a cold winter's night.

News had broken amongst the Tempusmancers that a large group of Necromancers were to ascend on the bustling community and take all known Tempusmancers that resided there. The takedown of Master Melvin was to be especially reserved for his brother, for the bitter sweetness of it all. Younger ones – those in training and had vulnerable powers – were either hidden or sent away to safe havens; to this category, Hans fell. Melvin had made him promise that he would stay in the false floor until he had received advice that it was over. Hans had begun to protest but was beaten by a single word: Go.

The war had started when a sudden quietness filled the streets, and each of the dim streetlights had gone out.

One. By. One.

It wasn't a normal quiet either. It was an eerie, high-tension quiet; the sort that you could hear a pin-drop at the other side of the street. The Necromancers brought stillness, brought death with them, and tonight it had descended on top of this unsuspecting community.

Hans listened, the throbbing of his heart ringing in his ears. Like this he waited for an hour.

For two hours.

For three.

He couldn't hear anything, so he creaked open the loose floorboards which served as the entry to the false floor and peeped through the crack.

The room was how it was left. Neat. Warm. Untouched.

Scanning the room, he pulled himself out of his hiding place when he realised no one was inside, and crouched down. He opened the curtains just a sliver so he could look outside of the second-storey window. Two figures stood in the snow outside, both bearing resemblances to each other. One of them was Master Melvin. The other was his brother.

The whole thing was over in a blink of an eye. The estranged brother had lunged for Melvin who in turn, attempted to feint. But the bluff was caught, and Hans watched as a long, dirty dagger was sunk into his Masters heart and twisted. Red liquid tainted the snow around them, and Melvin fell lifelessly with the snow beginning to bury his body.

There were things you can't change no matter how hard you try.

Hans gasped. He had once again lost someone that was family. Master Melvin had assumed the father role in his life and Hans had loved him as such. Restraining the tears in his eyes, he continued looking outward at the horrible, snowy scene.

As if hearing him, the estranged brother went rigid, reared his head and stared up at the second-storey window. He seemed to be staring directly at Hans, almost as if making eye contact. He withdrew the blade and, in a haunting manner, pointed at him through the window and slid a gloved finger along his own neck.

The brother smiled as Hans seemed to have interpreted the message correctly.

He was next.

- - -

"And what happened next?" asked Ellen, awestruck by Hans Greys' detailed recount.

She saw a faint smile spread across the man's lips, softness filling his eyes.

"Nothing. Nothing happened. This photograph," he pointed back at the book, "was taken after I had assumed Master Melvin's position on the Grand Committee. At this time, I was Grand Master but gave it away as it was a great burden and needed full commitment."

There was an awkward silence. Ellen wanted to hug the man for going through so much and to comfort him.

"Why did you share this with me?" she asked instead.

"I shared it with you because you need to understand the importance and impacts of your actions, but to especially highlight the great importance in being aware of your surroundings and how you need to keep what you are, a secret. There are bad Necromancers on the prowl, and there is a rumour that his brother is still out there hunting for people like us. If you can agree to be cautious, to be quiet, then I am happy to begin teaching you so you can help others. This is after all, what Tempusmancers were intended to do with their powers."

Ellen sat back in her chair, turning around so she was now facing Hans. It was clear that what was given to her was a dangerous gift, one that could threaten her life. On the flip side, it was something she could use to make the world a better place. Her head throbbed from the horde of thoughts that now clogged her mind and she found herself drowning in an anxious sweat. Would she find herself in a similar position to Hans and lose people she loved? Did she really have the potential that Hans saw in her? It was a major risk, one that would shape her future, no doubt.

Biting her lip, she gave her answer.

Chapter Five

The silence was bated and intense as Ellen stared at Hans, the type of silence you would expect when you see a performer walking a tightrope in front of a large audience. But there was no audience here. It was just the young, innocent girl and the former Grand Master of the Tempusmancers in an empty bedroom, in a common suburban home, in a well-off neighbourhood.

She continued staring at him through weary, agonising eyes, her teeth biting into the soft skin of her lips. Her desk lamp gave her a yellow, ghost-like tinge to her skin which made her look ill. Was she getting ill? Or was it just the effect of the proposition he gave her? Her stomach gave a jolt from the anxiety that rushed her. It felt as if she was caught between a rock and a hard place.

In fact, that's exactly where she was.

Ellen took the moment to mull over the choice she was given. It was between resuming her ordinary life as a teenager and pursue her dream or to live her life as a time-influence of sorts. She closed her eyes and began to speak.

"Hans..." she paused. "I really appreciate that you see potential in me but I don't think I could live that life. It's dangerous and what if it puts my family or friends at risk?"

The man sighed, an indication of resignation.

"I understand," he said simply. "Some people aren't built for this life." He turned around and straightened his clothes. He looked back at Ellen.

"In that case, the Grand Committee will begin the process of revoking your Tempusmancer practicing abilities. This should be within two weeks. In those two weeks if you feel the need to contact me, just imagine yourself talking to me in your mind. I will add that after that period, you won't remember a thing." He peered at her for a moment longer. Suddenly, he turned on his heel and left the bedroom through the ajar door. As if by automatic reflex, Ellen fled after him but by the time she burst into the dark hallway and ran to the head of the stairs, Hans had already disappeared without a single sound.

She sunk to her knees, head in hands, with her hair falling around her and creating a veil. She felt guilty for letting him down; the fact that he had divulged so much information to her. The nausea she felt ate at her, threatening to make her physically sick.

Tears rolled down cheeks, the first drop hitting the hallway carpet and darkening the area within seconds.

- - -

Three figures waited impatiently in the dark, unbeknownst to Ellen, across the road from her home. Excitement grew between them at what they had overheard and the decision the girl had made. This would please their superior greatly, maybe even to the point of being rewarded. As ruthless as he was, he always rewarded great help.

They had remained at their observation posts for a large portion of the day, watching as Ellen came home on her bicycle; her and her family having dinner, her reading the book and Hans appearing behind her. It was difficult to stay idle for such a long period of time and pretend they were city workers tending to the gardens. No one took double glances at city workers, they seemed to blend in to their surroundings. But it had paid off when the man left post haste, and they were able to ditch the disguises as soon as night had fell so long as they stayed out of sight.

The smallest man grew overbearingly impatient and was the first to break silence. "Do you think we should let him know?" He had a weak voice, and high-pitched like a mouse.

"He has his ways. He probably already knows and is making his way here," the second man replied, his tone implying boredom. Although the man that spoke first was a new convert, he had an unruly habit of grossly underestimating the power of their fearless superior. The second man took a glance at the third – and final – member of the small party. "What do you think?"

"He knows," the last of the men answered meanwhile, twirling a stick in his fingers and eyes glued to the house. "He knows for sure."

"And you should be grateful you are serving him," added the second man.

"But he's on the other side of the world, how can h-." The first man froze in mid-sentence, his eyes widen open in fright. A cool breeze had picked up and rustled the leaves of a nearby tree. It was enough to penetrate the trio's clothes, send chills down their backs, and make their breath visible. The long, grey metal street-lights that lined the street flickered and diminished, plunging the street into perpetual darkness. No one could see a single thing apart from the lights that remained on in the houses and if any of the residents took the chance to look outside, they would be blinded by the darkness. It was like staring at a plain piece of black cardboard. This was followed by deathly silence; the owls that were hooting earlier had stopped singing their song.

"How can I be here?" someone mused in front of them. There was a crisp click! of fingers and the street-lights came back at half-power, the light only enough to faintly show the charming newcomer. He was wearing elaborate Necromancer's robes; a robe made of dark, ivy green silk with gold trimming on the edges that illuminated from the scarce light. His skin was pale, his cheeks rounded, and his nose snubbed. His eyes were onyx black, and his hair was short; black with a gloss-like shine.

"Lord Lucien!" greeted the trio hastily; the smallest man gasping at the sudden presence of their superior.

His resemblance to his brother, Melvin, was undeniable. The resemblance was so close that they even shared the same smirk. Lucien stood in front of the three men, his arms crossed across his chest. He took striding steps towards the smallest of the men, the one that had questioned his abilities. The man immediately looked down at his shoes and refused to make eye contact. Lucien detected guilt, the heartbeat of the man standing before him ringing quickly and thunderously in his ears.

"Do you doubt me, commoner?"

"No, my Lord," he mumbled. Lucien saw the man sway minutely backwards, like he was trying to put more distance between them. He somehow doubted that it was intentional, more like an automatic flight or fight reaction. "One would not doubt a man of your calibre."

"Was it not you that questioned my whereabouts?" his voice was sharp, cutting into the man like swords. He was cowering in front of Lucien now. The remorse pleased him. It meant that his hard-earned authority still instilled fear into those around him.

"Yes, my Lord. But you are great. I need to be punished for my doubt."

A cold smile broke across Lucien's pale lips, making the hairs on the man's body stand on end. He adopted a soft voice, soft but blood-curdling. "Again, and I will take your firstborn that your wife is carrying at this moment. Is this clear in that thick skull of yours?"

The man nodded furiously. "Thank-you, my Lord, thank-you. You have been the most gracious."

Lucien lifted a hand and slipped two fingers underneath the man's chin. He lifted it so the man was now forced to stare into Lucien's burning eyes. "I promise you that, commoner. Mark my very words." He then dropped his fingers away. "Update on the situation, please," he requested from the others.

The third man, named Ratch, cleared his throat.

"The girl hasn't left the house since she came home from school and the library. Grey paid her a visit earlier this evening before you arrived and offered her mentoring to train her abilities. She rejected him and...," Ratch laughed, "he disappeared."

"Did he vanish? Inside the house?"

"Yes, my Lord. He hasn't stepped in or out of those doors. Dermott and his team can confirm that he hasn't accessed the rear door either."

"I'll get to Dermott after I finish with you three." Lucien paused, glancing downwards at the grass. He was evaluating scenarios that played out in his mind, scenarios which would help achieve what he had planning ever since the girl was born. His fingers shook as he analysed these scenarios.

"If Melvin's pet was able to vanish himself within the building, it means that it isn't protected by his network. It means we can access the building and carry out what we had intended to do. If it was protected, he would have had to remove himself outside to pull a vanishing act. The chances of it being protected would be slim however, as the girl technically isn't one of them," he spoke to himself. The other man looked onwards, afraid to interject. "That is. Not yet. The moment she agrees to change, each building she will be in will be protected making it harder to accomplish anything."

Ratch gazed onwards at Lucien, catching on to what his superior was eluding to.

"You're saying," he began. "That we do the snatch tonight as planned?"

"Correct. We do it tonight."

The other two men nodded their heads in agreement. Snatching the girl was inevitable, every Necromancer knew that. She possessed greater power than any of the Tempusmancers' ever had. If they were to make any progress in adopting these powers, the Necromancers had to get a hold of this girl and use her for life-changing – ground breaking – research. Once this was successful, the Necromancers would be able to gain different abilities that many of them only dreamed about. They could overcome their counterparts.

When he was just a student, Lucien's mentor had explained to him that a fabled prophecy had described that such a powerful being was only born once every century. All the details that had been given were accurate to what Lucien had observed about this girl; this girl that Grey was trying to transition to a Tempusmancer.

Lucien cleared his throat. "I need to confer with Dermott and his brethren. I will come back for you when it's time." He cast a quick glance up at Ellen's window and silently trekked along the fence-line that marked her property's boundary. With expert stealth agility, he jumped over the gate that divided the front yard and the back and crouched down, listening for movement and heartbeats. Finding what he was searching for, he cut his way through two tall bushes into a small gap between the bush line and fence. Another three men stood there, expectantly.

"Good evening, Lord Lucien," they acknowledged.

"Hello. Ratchs' team told me that Grey didn't enter or exit through the rear. Is that correct?"

A squat man with shaggy, shoulder length brown hair stepped forward. He was dressed in dark colours, to match in with his surroundings without a doubt. "That is correct."

"Did anyone come outside?" enquired Lucien. His voice was urgent. He had to know finer details if he was to make the move tonight, and time was something they didn't have much of. It was highly risky, especially if that Tempusmancer Grey had a hand in things. A tall, swallow man from behind Dermott stepped forward, him too dressed top to toe in darkness. He propped himself up against the back fence. He had a thick accent. A European.

"A nanny took their rubbish out. She looked like she was about to get a visit from death shortly. She was old and could barely move; not a threat."

Lucien snapped his face up at the unexpected news. "A nanny did you say?"

"Yup. As old as they come. Surprised she didn't have a walking stick. She must've gone home for the evening because we didn't see her go back in."

Rage erupted in Lucien. "Are you stupid?" he hissed, his face contorted in sheer anger. Hostility took over his body; his voice, his mind. The three men backed up towards the fence, away from their enraged superior.

"They don't have a nanny, you donkey!" Lucien spat at them. He motioned at Dermott. "You. Come here. NOW."

Dermott, his legs appearing to be made of jelly and his breathing becoming heavier by the second, stepped towards Lucien as if he was a drunkard. He drew himself up to full height and stood straight and rigid.

"Lord Lucien," he bowed his head, his voice grave.

"Did I not tell you that Grey is an illusionist? Did I not tell you that he could employ a disguise if he so needed?"

Dermott whimpered under Lucien's height, under Lucien's intimidation. "Yes, my Lord. But in our defence, she – him – was not distinguishable. 90 years old at least, heartbeats that were slow; you could hear fragility in her bones! She – HIM! – was everything a 90 year old should be! You didn't warn us against old women!" Dermott instantly regretted what he said the moment the last sentence slid from his mouth.

Lucien gripped the man's wrist and he immediately felt hellfire beginning to burn internally within him. He became paralysed.

"Do you have a wife?" Lucien snarled. The man nodded as a reply. The burning stopped and he regained control of his body. "Consider her perished. Learn from your mistakes or you too will join her," he threatened. He eyed the other two men that stared on in horror.

"Keep this idiot in line. Another one and you will both suffer for his mistakes. When you work as brethren, you take responsibility for each other."

The anger was still well and alive in his body as he made his way back to Ratch's men. Where did we find these sorry excuses? he pondered. The lacking quality in modern recruits was depressing, nothing like the men that were found centuries ago. He had to do something about it, a purge amongst the ranks. He saw Ratch waiting for him, underneath the shallow shadow cast by a large tree.

"Oh dear me," Ratch clucked, drawing out each word in a deep tone. "Aren't we in trouble?"

"They let Grey go. He pulled an illusion and vanished outside of the house."

"Do we make the move? Risk that it could be protected?"

Lucien stood quietly for a minute. Two minutes. Three minutes. So much planning went into this to just throw it away, the thought of it alone pained him. He answered on impulse; on what he deemed to be right.

"Yes. But we need to be prepared. Something tells me that Grey won't be too far away the moment he realises something is happening." Lucien turned to the second man, Hawk. "Will you do the honours?"

Hawk stood up from where he was sitting, clasped his two hands together and blew into them three times; three bursts of loud owl calls. This would signify to the others that it was time.

The front trio joined Lucien as they marched their way across the hard, bitumen road. Skulking along the side of the fence to avoid the crunching driveway, they lightly stepped onto the brilliantly polished wooden decking of the veranda. Taking the locked doorknob into his hands, caressing it like a handshake, the lock popped and the men crossed the threshold into the dark lounge room. It was clean, unlike Lucien's den. To his pleasant surprise, he didn't feel the sensation that usually washed over someone when protection was enforced. Not one of his men was falling to their knees, withering in pain.

Knowing the proceedings from the back of their minds, they crept into their positions. The front brethren were to assist Lucien upstairs with the girl whilst the brethren from the backyard were to secure the ground floor against any intrusions. Expecting the worst - a contingency of Tempusmancers - to come, Lucien had assembled the most brutal of his Necromancers to take the ground positions. They were young but they had strength and physical savagery needed to take the others down.

He led the way up the stairs, one at a time, with no creaking. Reaching the top flight, he looked into the main bedroom where her parents were sleeping. Ellen's father was snoring a storm, and his mother wasn't far behind him. Mumbling something under his breath, he made certain that they wouldn't wake up for at least five hours.

Five hours of deep slumber, he laughed. That's if you wake up by the end of it. I never quite mastered that yet. He then crossed the landing to where Ellen's bedroom was and noticed that the door was ajar and light was pouring from the gap. He could hear the rustling of pages and the compression of bedsprings.

Signalling for his preferred trio to stop at the stairs, he pulled out the oldest, grandest book he had in his library from beneath his robes and held this in his hands. He slipped a beautiful rose inside the top cover; something that he couldn't resist and knocked on the wooden door.

He turned back to his men for a last glance. Such a charming ladies' man, bringing flowers, Ratch mouthed at him. Rolling his eyes, Lucien pushed open the door and walked inside.

Ellen looked up from her bed and saw a man in robes walk into her room. His black hair gleamed in the light from the desk lamp, his pale skin contrasted against deep green and gold metallic robes. There was a certain handsome charm to him. He was holding an ancient book in his hands. The book she had borrowed from the library that was propped on her knees fell between her legs as she pulled herself off the bed and onto her feet.

"Who- who are you?" she stammered; her voice faulting. Was he part of the Grand Committee, here to take her abilities away? She looked back at the tissues that littered her bed.

"I understand you have rejected Hans Grey's offer? I'm here from the Grand Committee to get your final view on matters before we proceed forward," he said, gently. Sweetly. Innocently. Reassuringly.

"I've been thinking about that..."

"Oh. You have?" he smiled. There was something about him that made Ellen feel comfortable, as if he was an old friend. He took a few steps towards her and sat down in her desk chair. "And what did you think about?"

Ellen watched as he placed the heavy book onto her desk, a blood-red rose peeking out from the top. Odd, she thought to herself. She watched him smile, and this was pushed out of her thoughts.

"I want to be one of you."

There. She said it.

"Well, that's great news!" he enthused, placing his hands lightly on his crossed knees and smiling widely. He picked himself up from the chair and ambled towards her, placing a hand around her shoulders and rubbing her back for support. Ellen's nose prickled as she caught his scent; something summery, something flowery and earthy. She didn't have time to scream as he whipped his other hand around her mouth and nose so she couldn't breathe. Panic riddled through her body, anxiety rearing its ugly head as her body became deprived of air.

She tried pushing him off but he was too strong and easily overpowered her, grasping her into a lock.

"Shhhh, beautiful," he cooed in her ear, brushing a strand of hair away from her eyes. His touch was soft. "I promise you this won't be painful if you don't fight, darling." Ellen stared at disbelief at how calm the man was, his lips still in a friendly smile.

She clenched her eyes shut, as tight as she could.

Hans Grey. Where are you? I need you, she begged with her remaining energy.

And then she blacked out.

Chapter Six

Ellen opened her eyes, her vision out of focus and hazy. Her head was pulsing but she couldn't rub her temples; her hands were bound by thick, heavy chains that clanged on the stone tiling underneath her as she attempted to move. Her feet were also in shackles. As she regained her sight, she took a glance at her surroundings although she wished she hadn't and had kept her eyes closed. It was akin to a dungeon, and it appeared as if it came from the middle of a horrible experimentation laboratory.

It reignited her anxiety.

She was perched on the cold, hard stone floor which was damp and covered in moss and brown splatters.

Dried blood.

The four walls that towered over her were made from the same quarried stone as the floor, each block stacked precariously on top of the other. Light was being emitted from a single, bare light globe that flickered on and off. A heavy, reinforced metal door stood across the floor from her, closed and assumed to be locked.

Am I underground? she wondered to herself, all alone in this empty room.

Roots sprouted at odd angles from the crevices formed between the individual stone blocks, and water trickled down the block faces. There was a musky smell, very rich in earthly tones. This was mixed with something much more vulgar and sterile but she pushed this out of her mind. She didn't want to know but she had the suspicion that she would find out, anyway, with time.

Ellen gazed upwards at the roof. It was made of wooden panelling, this too caked in moss and leaking water. There was a plop! as each drop fell into a small puddle. Several of the slats were becoming bowed from the wetness and the compounding pressure coming from the top. It was an old room, and suffered greatly from neglect. It was a marvel that it was still intact.

She swallowed hard as she comprehended its scarce furnishings.

At the far end against the wall, there was a metal work station with a myriad of tools hanging above it. Knives, saws, hammers; they were all there, and they were all filthy and rust-riddled. In the centre of the room, below the bare bulb, was the centrepiece, an equally rusty surgeons table with heavy, leather restraining straps at both hands, feet and neck.

Ellen, now arriving back to her full senses, leaned the back of her head against the wall and closed her eyes. How foolish she was for believing a stranger that she had never seen before. She hit her head against the wall several times in disbelief, tears threatening to wet her cheeks. Because she had believed him, because she had been naïve, she ended up in this hell-hole.

She didn't want to die here.

With hope quickly fading like a flame without oxygen, she kept her eyes closed and wished – hoped – that Hans could hear her, track her down, feel her.

There was a metallic clink and a high-pitch squeal. She watched as the door slowly cracked open to expose two different people. The first was a tall, slender man in white doctor's robes with glasses and grey hair, who was immediately followed by the other man. The second man though, was familiar to Ellen. He was slightly shorter than the doctor and had cropped blonde hair with a slim face.

I know him. She squeezed her eyes shut, trying to rake through the memories and visuals that she could remember. Whilst she was in a frenzy, struggling to remember where she had seen him before, the two men conferred with each other, the doctor flicking his head in Ellen's direction and crossing his arms. The younger man sighed, and reluctantly made his way over to Ellen. Obviously unhappy with something, the man pulled a key from his pocket and yanked the heavy leg shackles off her. Her legs felt so, so light with that weight lifted.

"Get up," he snarled at Ellen, barely moving his lips. She didn't move.

"I said get up," he directed her again, the snarl even more sinister. And then suddenly, he slapped Ellen across the face and she bit the inside of her mouth. Where he hit her grew red and began to sting, and she tasted something salty in her mouth. Tears started collecting under her eyes. "No more smart comments otherwise you get another one."

"What do you think you are doing?" someone asked. The calm and collected tone was a stark contrast again the other man's coarse growl. "We need her in good shape, not battered and bruised. She's special. Handle her with care. Unless... you can't even do a simple job like that?"

The tall man that captured her in her bedroom appeared, leaning up against the doorway. He seemed to be at ease, his face showing not the slightest hint of emotion. Pushing himself away from the metal frame, he wandered to where Ellen was still sitting and crouched down so they were now eye-to-eye. His breath brushed against her cheeks and his nose nearly touched hers. He stared intensively for just a moment longer and then looked up at the other man and said "You're dismissed." The man walked away and joined the doctor, leaving Lucien and Ellen alone.

Ellen felt bitter hatred towards the man that now crouched in front of her and refused to look at him. Her nostrils flared as she let out forceful streams of air, the result of anger and disgust.

Come on Hans, she wished, desperately. Where are you?

"I apologise for that," he told her, using that same charming, innocent voice he used in the bedroom when he made the snatch. "Some people don't have very good social skills." Lucien saw a clump of mud stuck to Ellen's hair and pulled it out, dumping the clump next to him. Ellen faltered as he made contact with her. He had a small smile on his face, a smile that was enough to strike fear inside her. She sensed the power and air of authority that this man which made her dread him even more.

"Would you like me to help you get up?" he eyed the hand shackles on her wrists and laughed at the sight of them, his laugh warm yet gently eating away at her psychologically. "I imagine they would be quite heavy on those fragile hands of yours." Thoughtfully, he extended his hands and gently took her by the forearms. His touch was soft, hauntingly soft, and she was surprised that he was actually warm to the touch. Someone so evil could only be cold hearted with no ounce of warmness at all.

"Come on now, carefully. That's it, that's it." He supported her by the underarms and spent a minute observing her. Dirty, muddy blonde hair, a t-shirt and short shorts that were stained with filth, skin that was covered in mud. Ellen felt his eyes pierce through her, analysing every little detail right down to her feet. She felt the energy wane from her body involuntarily as she resigned to her fate. He put his arm underneath again and guided her to the surgeons table.

"I promise you," he told her reassuringly. "That this won't hurt at all, my dear. Now, if you just sit down," he helped her onto the cold metal surface. "And we put your feet up like this," he lifted her feet and placed them down carefully. Ellen was unable to fight against it, her body unreceptive to movement. "Then that is all you have to do. You have been a very good girl." She watched on as he winked at her and flashed a wide grin.

"Just one more thing because we don't want you falling off, do we?" He held down each of her hands and feet as he tightened the straps around them firmly, deciding to forgo the one for the neck. The leather straps cut into her skin, much more than the shackles had. She began to cry, overcome by fear, the torture, and the psychological anguish that was taking place. He peered down at her, the smile disappearing.

"Oh, dear. No. No. It's okay, don't cry. You'll be okay. It won't hurt, will it Doctor?" He wiped away the wetness that ran down her face. He looked away to the side at the white-robed doctor but she couldn't see him. He was well outside of her peripheral vision. There were footsteps from somewhere behind her, the noise echoing in the dungeon.

"Not one bit," the elderly man replied. She watched as the doctor gave the man a syringe of clear liquid. It suddenly hit her that the man that had struck her earlier was the man that was crushed between the two cars! How was this possible? He should have been dead! That's why he was chasing her. To try and catch her he but he failed.

"This," her snatcher showed her. He kept the psychologically tormenting demeanour as he spoke. "Will put you into a happy place whilst we take a look at you." Ellen tried to scream but it was stuck in her tightened throat. She opened her mouth, nothing coming out, gaping like a fish out of water. She tried to push away with her feet but the straps held her in place. He ran a finger along the bend in her arm, stroking it. Then he dropped down lower and lifted the needle closer to it. Taking a look at her, he slowly sunk it underneath her skin and depressed the contents into her vein. He stood back up straight and gazed down into her eyes. Ellen felt light, as if her body had been detached and she was floating. She drifted in and out of a dream - a blissful dream - and continued to look back at him as she fell into a trance like state. The last thing she remembered was the man raising an arm and pushing her hair away from her face. He bent down and kissed her forehead softly.

And that was when she closed her heavy eyelids.

Lucien stood there for a lingering moment longer, satisfied that they had finally got the girl. She looked peaceful, unknowing that the next time she woke up, she wouldn't be the same.

"Would you like to watch, or will you be leaving my Lord?" asked the doctor, distracted. He grabbed a sharpening block and pulled a long blade along it. His eyes grew shiny as the blade got sharper with each pull.

"I think I will leave and let you do the honours, dear friend. You've been preparing for this day for the last century." Lucien left the room with a backward glance. Soon. They were the closest they have ever been.

Soon.

- - -

The elderly doctor was mid-process of preparing his tools when the solid, metal door to the chamber opened once again. The grubby man that had struck Ellen across the face reappeared, huffing and in a foul mood. The doctor, amused by his behaviour, cast a sideward look. "What's with you?"

The sulky man leaned supported himself on the workbench, looking onwards at the doctor. "He's not particularly happy about my handing of her. But she wasn't following my direction, you see? You know where I'm coming from?"

The doctor sighed and placed the tools he was holding down. "She's important. It's crucial she's intact." He squinted at the man's hands. What appeared to be fresh blood was on them. He took a quick waft, and this was confirmed by the smell that filled his nostrils. "What did he do to you?"

"Oh," the man began, face falling. "He didn't do anything but I had to take care of something upstairs."

The doctor raised an eyebrow. The man's story not making any sense. They never did any sort of blood-drawing upstairs. It was too dirty for Lucien's standards. He opened his mouth, but – by no control of his own – closed it. The man now turned, his whole body facing the doctor. His cropped, blonde hair had disappeared and was now replaced by long, silver locks. He was taller, thinner, and his features were more chiselled than before.

"Grey," hissed the doctor. Realising that the he had been tricked and Grey was here to save the girl, the doctor made a rash decision and seized the closest, sharpest instrument he could find. He sprinted to the bed where Ellen was laying. He raised it and rammed it home roughly where her heart was. Little did he know that he was a few centimetres off target. One of these powerful creatures was born every hundred years. What would another hundred year wait be? Blood poured from the wound and pooled onto the metal table.

Enraged, Hans closed the distance in a number of strides and grasped the doctor by his neck. He kicked out a foot that intersected with the back of the doctors knees and he went down, heavier than a sack of bricks. Grabbing the doctor like a rag-doll, he pulled him up so the helpless doctor was now on his knees.

"You made a bad," Hans spat at the man. "Bad move." He placed a hand on his forehead and the doctor slumped backwards lifelessly, coming to a still sprawl on the filthy, stoned floor.

Ignoring this lump of skin and bones, he frantically felt down Ellen's body to detect whether she was alive. She was drugged heavily but there was still a weak pulse. Hopefully, he thought to herself. His anger grew as he saw the straps cutting into her skin, now leaving red markings against the paleness. He reached to the buckles and each flipped open, releasing her. Knowing it was only a matter of time – time that was slipping through his fingers – before Lucien became aware of what was happening, he scooped the limp Ellen into his arms and exited the room. His time-controlling abilities were stripped inside this compound which made him vulnerable, so he took extra-precaution to avoid as many Necromancer's as possible and started to retrace his steps.

He saw the stairwell at the end of the hall that he now stood in, relieved that he was outside of what could only be described as a torture chamber. The hall wasn't very different in terms of darkness, but the stone walls were clean and the floor was replaced with panelling. It hinted of the grandeur of the floors above. He made his way up the stairs, his footsteps light against the wooden floor. He was met by greater light as he reached the top. Hans then stepped from the staircase and into an elaborate entrance room. Large windows provided panoramic views of outside although, now, it was the darkness of the wee-early morning hours. Hans spied the door that would lead him out of the building.

Safety was just outside of those doors and beyond the gates.

Wanting to get away as soon as possible, he hurried across the room and erupted under the eaves of the façade. It suddenly occurred to him that this entire journey had been easy, a little bit too easy. He only had to dispose of two Necromancer's: one that had try to trap him when he entered the compound, and the other being the elderly doctor that had stabbed Ellen. The girl was still limp in his arms and had stopped bleeding. His clothes were drenched but he would deal with that later – it was the least of his problems. He stepped onto the gravel of the driveway that would take him beyond the wrought-iron gates, to the point that he would be able to vanish, and started to walk down.

Had Lucien anticipated this? Did he direct his path to be clear so he could deal with him himself? He wouldn't put it past Lucien to sacrifice his men if needed, even if they had served him loyally for years. And it didn't seem possible that Lucien would not be aware that he was here. Hans felt himself go cold. The brother, the killer of his Master, was here. And Hans was a mere few steps from freedom.

"I was expecting you," came a familiar voice, a chuckle added in for good measure. "I knew you would come to rescue the mortal girl. How... noble of you."

"I wish I could say as much for you," Hans replied simply. He turned on the heels of his feet so he was facing Lucien, Ellen swaying in his arms. Lucien stood twenty metres in front of him, his features the same from the very night Hans so distinctly remembered. It appeared he hadn't aged a single day.

"Look at you. Pathetic. Putting your life on the line for a girl. So heroic. Just like your Master was before he died." His empathy made Hans sick but he fought it, and he fought it hard.

"Says the person interfering with the dead, and killing his own just to attain greater power. Your teacher must be proud." Lucien flinched and Hans pressed on. "But that's right. You got rid of him too."

"I knew you were trouble when I saw you through that window."

"Then why didn't you finish me?"

"Because the chase is better than the catch." There was silence as the two men stared at each other, emotions tense from the past and the present. Metaphorically, it was as if good was versing evil but this wasn't the case. It was about the struggle for power; power that came down to a single girl that was cradled in Hans' arms and had potentially lost her life. Instinctively, Hans sprinted for the wrought-iron gate line as Lucien lunged for him. Dodging his outstretched hands, Hans stepped across the invisible line and knew that he had his full abilities reawakened.

Catching a glimpse of Lucien's contorted, raging face, Hans visualised his destination and made the connection he required to be successful. He made a step, as if setting himself up for a sprint, and he felt himself fall through the ground. He closed his eyes. When his feet had landed on solid ground, he opened them and knew he was safe; at least, for the time being. Hans placed the motionless and cold body of Ellen onto a nearby bed, his thoughts in a scattered mess.

Did he make it in time to save her?

He didn't know.

Chapter Seven

Hans sat on a padded armchair next to the bed where the still-bodied Ellen lay, the stab wound from the wretched doctor a dark brown. The iron in the blood had oxidised. His head was in his hands and his long silver hair fell to the floor. His face was contorted in frustration, or was it guilt? He couldn't distinguish the two, nor could he even bare to take a single glance at her. Whatever the feeling was, it was eating away at his body for leaving her alone. If she wasn't alone, if he hadn't turned his back, this wouldn't have happened. He would have been there to protect her from the Necromancers.

In his haste to leave the compound and put distance between them and the twisted Lucien, the first destination he could think of to vanish to was the inner-rooms of the Grand Committee manor. Although he had resigned as the Grand Master a good time ago, he still held a high rank, enough authority and prestige to be classified as a senior member and gain access to all the rooms within the building. At times of duress, the manor also proved to be one of the safest places, stripping Necromancers from all their power and allowing

Tempusmancers to keep theirs. It provided an advantage that Necromancers knew all too well and kept them away from attacking within the constraints of the manor.

On his arrival and after describing the events that had unfolded, the Grand Committee had ushered them into one of the private healing rooms; rooms that were positioned close to the nurse's quarters and that were tended to on a routine basis. An aged Tempusmancer was already waiting for them when they had arrived, an expert in wounds inflicted by Necromancers and their weapons. She took a look at the wound and determined that the blade the doctor had used wasn't made of any special materials which would require intensive aftercare. She did however, give an ultimatum to Hans about saving the girls life – he would either have to finish converting her so she had full powers or let her be human and she would succumb to the wounds. When she had delivered this news, she squeezed Hans on the shoulder, solemnly, and left the pair alone so he could deliberate. Now, he sat in the armchair weighing up his options.

The healing room they were in was a comfortable environment, much like what he needed. Its drapes of cream, its off-white walls, and plush carpeting allowed him to relax and feel like he was at home whilst he continued to be construed in thought. A light, summery scent was periodically sprayed into the room, giving the light room a natural feel. Two large, padded armchairs were placed beside the bed, there in anticipation for a greater number of guests. It was in one of them where he sat now. He worked hard to slow his rapid thoughts, trying to make sense of them all. He was at a loss of what to do; what the right decision was. It added to the frustration he was now feeling.

Only a short time ago, Ellen had refused the conversion and the Grand Committee was put on alert to revoke any remaining powers she had left. She didn't want to be subjected to the fights, to the deaths and danger that came with being a Tempusmancer. Inevitably, he did partly bring her amidst it. Almost instantly, he sensed that she regretted this decision and that was when the Necromancers made their move. They preyed on her at her most vulnerable, and betrayed her trust. Now, she was lying next to him, bordering death and her pulse weakening every minute that went by. If she was converted, she would be finding herself in the middle of what she was trying to avoid. If he didn't do anything, she would lose her life but she wouldn't be able to fall back within Lucien's grasp and the Necromancers would have to wait another century to seek greater power.

Hans glanced back at the blonde haired girl, his face turned into a frown, and mentally called for the Grand Master. He had to get an opinion on this; it had the potential to later impact the entire race and he wanted to make sure he was making the right choice. He saw the door to the room open silently from the corner of his eyes within a minute and then it closed.

"You called?" a voice asked. An austere looking woman stood inside of the door, her hands in front of her and folded neatly within each other. Long, glistening black hair sprouted from the top of her head and ended mid-way down her back. Her face was slim and portrayed youthfulness, and her body was draped in deep-maroon drapes. Electric blue eyes gazed from behind narrow-rimmed glasses. Although seemingly young, Hans knew too well that she was in his senior. Her voice was calculating and deliberate.

"Claudia," Hans emitted weakly. His head was still in his hands. He was aware that he must've looked like a schoolchild – the once great Hans Grey – but he didn't care. He wasn't afraid to admit that he too had weak moments; moments where he needed guidance. "I'm at a loss."

Claudia walked – glided – silently across the room and took the seat next to Hans. She crossed her leg, her hands now folded on her knees. "I sense great conflict within you, Hans Grey." She peered down her nose, out of the glasses.

"For once in my life, I am lost," he sighed. He dropped his hands between his legs and slumped back into the chair. His body deflated and he appeared broken in mind, in spirit. Claudia analysed his face; the perplexity, the genuine worry that flooded onto this face. This was what once made him a great leader.

"My son," she began. "Why did you put your own life on the line if you are going to let this girl-child die?" The question grabbed Hans by the throat, the honesty of it being brutal and lashing at his aches. She pressed on. "You sit here before me, a wreck of sorts. You sit here doubting that you did the right thing. You sit here wondering if it's easiest to let her go. You sit here doubting her. You sit here doubting yourself."

Hans felt his heartstrings get tugged.

"Claudia," he acknowledged. He was truly lost for words.

"Hans Grey. You, of all people, should know that talent like this should be cherished and trained to be productive. When the time comes for another war, we will want all the talent we can afford to get and this girl is another prodigy who could advance our cause. She could advance us."

There was a twinkle in the woman's eyes as she knew that what she was saying was being absorbed by Hans.

"You know. I remember when Melvin first told us about a worthy prospect; I remember when he told us about you," she placed emphasis on each of these words. Not only did it stir Hans inside, but it stirred her too.

"He was excited that he found someone so capable of living our life that he was virtually skipping through our doors to tell us. After knowing that you had lost your parents and were an orphan, he took you in with the hopes of raising you as his own son. He was incapable of having his own. He genuinely thought that he could save you and you could save him. And in a way, you did. You taught him how to love and have compassion. He put his life on the line for you."

Deep inside, Hans knew what Claudia was alluding to, but it didn't protect him from its impact on his emotions.

"You have a choice in front of you to save someone that is as worthy of you. The answer is clear but ultimately, it is your decision alone. Just remember, Melvin was about making the world better. Don't make him be disappointed in you if he was still here." She fell silent, allowing her words to sink into Hans' mind.

He gazed at her through confused eyes, and took a massive breath. "Thank you for your clarity and wisdom."

Claudia sat for a brief moment more and grabbed his hands into hers. She gave them a squeeze – a warm squeeze – and left the room so he was left alone.

With a clearer mind and knowing what he had to do, he stepped up from the chair and neared the bed where Ellen lay. Hans sat on the side, the soft mattress sagging underneath his weight. He took her hands, just like Claudia did to his, and felt the coldness against his warmth. Bowing his head, he closed his eyes and started an incantation; the same incantation that was told to him by Melvin. It brought back a wealth of memories but he suppressed these to the back of his mind. The incantation was a solid two minute affair of nonstop muttering and was administered when the time was right to awaken full powers of new Tempusmancers. Of course, this was after they accepted conversion. The familiar tingling and warmth surged to his fingertips. The ritual was complete. Hans placed Ellen's hand gently next to her and shifted back to the armchair.

He wasn't sure of how long this process would take, or if it would be successful in saving her. It was the unknown and this ate away at him. Time trickled past, each second seeming like a lifetime. With growing impatience, he rose from the armchair and stood and paced the room absent minded. He never realised how quiet it could be; the quietness haunting him. His footsteps were muffled by the thick carpet, and it gave a soft of spring to his step. He could feel his temples throbbing from anticipation.

Back and forth.

Back and forth.

There was a clearing of a throat, and Hans jumped a few centimetres off the ground in surprise. The female doctor was standing in the doorway, a stethoscope hanging limply around her neck. She was attempting to stifle her laugh, the hint of a smile tugging at the corners of her mouth.

"I believe she's stirring, Hans." The words she uttered in her Irish brogue were musical to his ears; these words have never been so welcome. He whipped his head back at the girl and, sure enough, colour was returning to her drained skin. It was faint but it was definitely getting stronger. Ellen's cheeks were no longer ghastly white and now had a pinkish tinge. Her body had a healthy glow. Relief and happiness radiated from deep within his body.

"It could take a while for her to recover fully so I advise to give her space. Wait here if you must, but give her room," the doctor cautioned. She hurried to the bed, and placed her stethoscope on Ellen's chest. The beats were getting stronger but there were large improvements needed just yet. "I'll send in a Guardian to nurse and take care of her," she called to Hans. She continued to talk to herself, identifying what required doing. "She needs to get out of these clothes and into something clean. She needs those wounds patched up. She needs..." And then the doctor left, leaving Hans alone again, the quietness not as deafening as it was previously.

He wasn't left alone for long. Ellen's Guardian bustled through the door, holding an assortment of items thrown into a tub. He was young although this didn't make Hans doubt his skills. They were only designated as such if the individual had shown constant compassion, care, and dedication as a Tempusmancer. This specific Guardian had worked with Hans countless times, to the point they had established mutual respect.

"Hans," he acknowledged. He dropped the tub he was holding at the foot of the bed and tipped the contents out. Bandages, clothes, a clean change of clothes. He took the tub to a smaller side room and came back. The container sloshed with water every step he took, flecks of it being adsorbed by his shirt. He picked up a sponge and began to work on Ellen's wound and bathing her. The dirt and dried blood slowly disappeared, making the water a murky brown. Her clothes were stripped and changed to a clean t-shirt and pants. The Guardian had placed one finger on her face, preparing to delicately clean her face, when one of Ellen's fingers twitched. The movement spread like an electric surge to her whole hand and then she opened her eyes and her throat shifted.

"Him," she croaked. The two men stared at her, the Guardian dropping the sponge into the tub and shifting it away. Hans bent down close to her, their noses nearly brushing against each other.

"What about him?" he asked her, clearly and slowly.

"He nearly killed me. It hurts." Her voice was contorted with the pain and Hans felt helpless. Her eyes flickered open, exposing her light-brown eyes. They flitted at the Guardian and lingered, and then at Hans. She was still visibly weak but it was a vast improvement from where she had been. "He's a cop. He drove me home."

The Guardian smiled. "Only when I need to be."

Ellen remained neutral and then muttered words into Hans' ear, reigniting the guilt in him. "I don't trust anyone."

She then closed her eyes, still weak, and entered a deep, deep slumber; a slumber that took her away from reality for the time being.

Chapter Eight

Hans stirred in his armchair, listening to Ellen's heavy breathing as she continued to sleep close by. His nap was dreamless, much to his satisfaction. He twisted his neck to ward off the stiffness, and tried to get a sense of the time. It was nearing lunchtime meaning that he was asleep for longer than he thought. He rubbed his eyes and shifted in his armchair so he was now upright. He quickly came to realise that Ellen's parents were unaware of what had happened the previous night. They were probably worried, sick with fright, as to what happened with their daughter; their daughter whom was now missing from the family household. Deciding it best to scout the home before letting Ellen return and to determine the state of it, he refreshed himself in the side bathroom and prepared himself for the departure. Giving the girl a parting glance, he left through the door and alerted the young Guardian assigned to her that he will be away for a short stint of time. The young man nodded and wished him good luck on his travels.

Arriving in the main foyer, he closed his eyes and painted the destination in his mind. The white painted, double-storey home with flower beds framing the sweeping, gravel driveway. Having this planted firmly in his imagination, he took a purposeful step in front of him and felt himself suddenly weightless. Within a split second, his feet landed on the hard earth underneath him and he opened his eyes to the home from his visualisation towering over him. Hans concentrated, trying to detect any unusual movement or sounds coming from within the walls. Nothing.

He took long, sweeping strides to the doorway and let himself into the immaculately kept entrance hallway. It was as silent as a crypt; no noise, no footsteps or anything apart from the giant grandfather clock the family owned that was ticking away. He found this awkward. If someone's child had suddenly disappeared at the dead of night without your knowledge and disappeared the following morning, surely you'd call the police.

Right?

He craned his head around the doorway that led to the kitchen. Empty. The stainless steel appliances glimmered in the lunchtime sunshine that shone through the windows. It looked like it hadn't had breakfast cooked in it. The dish drying rack was empty, the tea towels hanging neatly from the handle of the oven. A lump got caught in his throat as his alertness began to rise. He fled the entrance hall and leaped up the stairway, two stairs at a time. His heart was heavy, and his blood pumping fast. He was familiar which was Ellen's bedroom and headed in the opposite direction, breaking into a run. The door was ajar to what he suspect was her parents' bedroom.

Pushing it open with the lightest push from the tip of his fingers, his gut instincts were confirmed although he wished they were wrong.

He lost control of his body and fell to his knees in a ragdoll-like heap. It was yet another blow to him. Lucien had struck once again, beating the once-great Hans Grey and turning Ellen into an orphan. He robbed her of the mere couple of years of innocent childhood she had left with her parents before turning eighteen. Hans already knew that Lucien had undertaken this deed himself, his traditional hallmarks all present. The mess of the execution and the appearance of struggling. Both of their bodies lay side by side and were barely distinguishable.

Hans stared onwards at the scene, feeling hollow, something small and white catching his eye. A folded piece of paper stood on a nightstand, appearing like it was purposefully placed there. He picked it up and opened it, only being met by a few words written in a flowy, cursive font: You can't protect everyone. He scrunched it up in his palm, the piece of paper now just a small, jagged ball. The note - those few words - seemed to act like a warning to Hans; an unspoken warning telling him to watch his steps. Those that knew Lucien were very familiar that he was a ruthless killer and wasn't an aficionado for taking prisoners.

With nothing else to keep him there and unknowing if he was being watched, Hans rushed out of the bedroom and down the staircase into the entrance hallway. He surged through the front door without a second glance and erupted onto the veranda of the large house. In a blink of an eye, he was gone.

"This has escalated much further than we initially forecasted."

A murmur of voices broke out and quickly died down, silence filled with anticipation descending on the room. There was a ruffle, scraping sound as uncomfortable bodies were being shifted in chairs. The entire Grand Committee, a coalition of twenty prominent Tempusmancers, had scrambled to meet within the large boardroom on the learning of Hans' findings. The room itself was expansive, lit only by candles. A large, antiquated table lined the middle of the room, surrounded by a number of equally as old chairs. Timeless gold treasures decorated the middle of the table, and commissioned portraits of influential leaders hung from the walls. At times, one almost felt as if these portraits stared at them, taking in their every move. This room was now filled with what was regarded as the most important and influential people of their time.

Hans was seated directly to the left of Claudia whom was at the head of the long table and next to him was the Guardian that was put in charge to look after Ellen. Both of them looked composed however the others were in various states of anger, shock and to some extent, panic. Claudia rapped her knuckles on the table, commanding attention from those around her that had started worrying with the people they sat next to.

"May I remind you," she said, threateningly and in the stern voice that a mother uses with their young, "that what Master Hans Grey has seen isn't necessarily the declaration of attack on our kind. They are after Miss Ellen who, may I add, we knew possessed incredible attributes which would be beneficial to us."

Further murmur arose in the room, quenched when another had started speaking, this time an elderly man. He was clearly one of the ones in the room that was wrought with panic.

"We weren't aware that converting her would be so dangerous! If we persist with protecting this girl, what would that spell for our respective clans? Why should we put our clans in danger for this girl?" There was a thunderous applause as those that agreed with him showed their support.

"I say Claudia, that this be put to a vote! She either remains protected at the risk of sacrificing members of our clans in wars or she be released and left to fight for her oneself! That way, we are in no danger. They are not after us after-all!" More applause followed. The man had a smile on his face, a smug one at that.

"This is not a vote that will happen under my steering, Master. Ellen is important to us, and we - yes, WE - as a collective will keep her safe. And I strongly urge you reconsider your allegiances for even suggesting we put one of own on the streets and forget about them. I expect more from you. Another utter like that, and your clan may find themselves needing a new leading Master," Claudia shot icily in the direction of the previous speaker. "Maybe you would be better aligned to Lucien's agenda, rather than our own?"

The effect the last question had on the room was close to earthshattering. Many of those on the committee gasped, a few had shrieked, and the belittled Master had spat in Claudia's direction. Han's had felt himself flinch and he noticed the Guardians hands turn white in his lap as he squeezed his own hands so tightly it was preventing blood circulation. A glass broke in the person that sat directly opposite him, the shards spraying across the table top.

"How dare you accuse me of such nonsense!" wailed the accused, who was on his feet now, finger pointing threateningly at Claudia's chest. His face was violently crimson; his eyes wide open.

"Sit down before you embarrass and make an idiot out of yourself in front of everyone." Her voice was calm, commanding. This was just part of the reason why she was admired by many.

Without being able to illicit the response he wanted, the man sat down and sunk deep into his chair, shrinking away from the others around him that were now suppressing giggles at how easily he was diffused.

"Shut up," he snarled to those that were within earshot.

"Master Hans Grey." Claudia turned to face him, her tone gentle and diplomatic. "Doctor Casey advised me that Ellen has been administered the incantation and has been fully converted and awakened, I understand. Is this correct?"

"Yes. This is correct." Hans bowed his head a sign of respect. Smiling, Claudia pressed onwards.

"As the administering Master, would you be willing to accept her into your clan, to tutor and to nurture her? To protect her to the best of your ability, knowing that we will be of aid if we are so required?" Her eyes darted to the man, squinted, and then back at Hans. "I believe this would be right up your alley."

"It would be an absolute honour."

"Guardian Roland, are you able to keep assisting?"

The Guardian next to Hans nodded curtly. "Of course, with pleasure."

The Grand Master clapped her hands together, joyfully. "Well, that's settled. I need to reiterate that if any of you see anything that constitutes an act of attack on your clans, that you advise me immediately so that action can be carried out promptly. Without a doubt, your people have heard rumours," another glance in the man's direction, "of what has happened. Remember to promote unity, calmness and cohesiveness to the greatest extent you can whilst being alert. We are all the same. Anyone leading their clans back in their respective locations otherwise will be dealt with according to protocol, as will those that act as double agents if we come under siege."

There was commotion in the room as Claudia was first to exit, followed by the rest in single file. Whilst all of them were happy with the outcome of the meeting, only one of them felt the need to vent outside of the boardroom walls: the Master that had ruefully suggested that they put Ellen on the street. His face was a lighter shade of crimson now - a light red - but his voice was still filled with bitterness and contempt. He was a short man in comparison to Hans, and he was well-rounded in the middle. A sausage-like arm was now outstretched to the side, supporting him against a wall. He was in an intense conversation with a female Master however, her face portrayed that she would rather be elsewhere and she made no effort at structuring conversational sentences.

"I don't see why everyone else has to be put at risk just because of one girl. Quite frankly, my clan will be outraged once I return. We don't stand for this sort of tosh! And the way she was drivelling, you'd think that this was the Hans Grey show! Scum couldn't even take top honours without derailing everything," he screeched, his hands flailing everywhere. As Hans walked past him, he had to dodge one of the man's escaped arms. They locked eye contact for a brief moment in passing; Hans sweeping away, his long robe bellowing behind him, and Rolland at his heels. The woman caught by the man's tirade gave him a small wave which he returned.

- - -

Over the months that had ensued, Hans started teaching and mentoring a fully-strengthened Ellen, much the same as his Master had once taught him as a child. But prior to being able to do this, he had had to have the inevitable, heart-wrenching discussion with Ellen about her parents. It had resulted in a very tearful evening and Hans stayed by her until dawn, both as a teacher and as a new-found friend; their shared experience consolidating a very special, unspoken bond. Darkness shadowed them both, like an old friend, but the darkness also gave her strength to push on. The following morning, Ellen had come to terms with the path her life and submitted herself to Hans' instruction.

Without haste, he began to teach her the charters and protocols they were bound by. This was followed by elementary time and fate control which started on a very basic level. When Hans was content that she could control her own powers without his constant vigilance, he escorted her to countless cafes and bars in various cities for what he liked to termed fun. Both of them took turns manipulating each patrons drink order and, at one point, Ellen influenced a squirm-ish young boy to buy a drink for the lady that he had been checking out from the corners of his eyes. Amused by her manipulations and fascinated at her ability to rapidly master the skill, Hans took her back to the manor and intensified his lessons.

As she progressed through his teachings and became more powerfully able, her variety of skills in her repertoire began to grow. Ellen was able to diffuse large, hostile situations; achieve acute hearing to the point she could hear blood flowing in peoples veins, and able to disguise her own appearance. She was reaching the stage that Claudia had started amassing interest in her, sitting in on several of Hans' lessons when she had the free time. In their initial meeting, Ellen had the impression that she was a formidable, strict woman and so she was. But she was also genuine and intelligent beyond comprehension.

During a particular wet morning, Ellen was already waiting in the practising room when Hans had entered and was followed closely by Claudia. She wasn't wearing her usual garments but rather donned a padded, high necked jacket, long legged tights and trainers.

"Claudia's taking you this morning," Hans informed Ellen with boredom, pulling a chair and sitting down. Ellen snapped her head to both of them, her mouth hanging wide open like a flytrap.

"What?" she gasped, shocked. She quickly apologised but saw that Claudia wasn't fazed by her reaction and was busy pushing tables and chairs against the wall. When she finished stacking the last chair, she turned to face them, obviously ready to start.

"I'm impressed by your ability to grasp our skills. I want to really put you to the test and let you attempt at things that are a bit more advanced," she said to Ellen, her eyes gleaming. "Some of the advanced things that even aged Tempusmancers have trouble doing."

"Oh?" Ellen's interest prickled up, like a dogs ears stand straight when listening to sound.

"Three things," she held up three gloved fingers. "Vanishing."

One finger was folded.

"Reading memories."

Another finger.

"Combat."

The last finger fell down like a toy soldier.

The tall woman stood over Ellen, almost threateningly. "Vanishing can have great consequences if done recklessly. Isn't that right Hans?" she shot at the man, who had busied himself reading a newspaper.

"Grapevine says that you have had a few... isolated incidents yourself," he chuckled to himself, poking his tongue out like a child so only Ellen saw. Claudia rolled her eyes, lost for words. The two of them bantered on for a few sentences more, leaving Ellen with the feeling that she wasn't sure if she wanted to know what Hans had spliced during his training.

"Now, Ellen. I want you to close your eyes and concentrate hard, the hardest you have ever done, on the other side of the room. Imagine it, imagine how it looks, how it smells even. In your mind, put yourself into that space." Ellen closed her eyes, trying with all her might to visualise the space. The panelled walls, the red carpeted floor, the smell of wood.

"Is it burned into your mind?" Claudia asked, her voice coming from somewhere behind her. Ellen nodded. "Good, good; let that flow through you for a second longer. Now, I want you to continue imagining that room and take a rushed step in front of you. As if you are preparing to take part in a sprinting competition. You're running for your life." Ellen did what was told, taking a brief moment to paint that room into her mind, and then took the step. For a moment she felt weightless, her feet leaving the floor. The following moment, only one of her feet had hit ground again and she opened her eyes. Yes, she was on the other side where she was supposed to be. But one of her legs wasn't. She looked down at her body in horror, one foot staring back at her.

Claudia's eyes furrowed a finger was on her lips. "We'll have to fix that."

By the end of that session, Ellen was able to vanish successfully without splicing her body though, vanishing with a companion was significantly harder and would come later. She had also witnessed a small number of memories from Claudia's Grand Master ceremony. Although they had attempted light combat - forcing Claudia to become paralysed - Ellen was unsuccessful, but was, nevertheless, congratulated on her solid efforts and achievements for the day. The trio were due to the servery for lunch but as they were leaving, Claudia requested Ellen to meet them there as she wanted a quick word with Hans in private.

Happily obliging, Ellen left the room, making her way down the hallway. As she was about to turn a corner, she heard a soft sobbing - begging - in one of the rooms; the sound floating from underneath the doorway.

"...please, no. Now is not the time...but Sire. You don't understand..." It was a man's voice, and it was petrified. It was also unlike anything that she had heard before nor recognised; alien-like, high-pitched wrought with fear, and weak. Feeling as if it was not her conversation to overhear, she pushed it to the back of her thoughts and went on her way without a second thought.

Chapter Nine

Hours had lapsed and the lightness outside of the curtains had begun to fade; the manor eventually swallowed by the darkness. The large shady trees the windows of the rooms opened to had fallen quiet for another day, the grounds were free of roaming groundskeepers, and large balls of warm-yellow light were slowly being turned on to illuminate the pathways linking smaller buildings to the main. The manor was a peaceful place and the beauty of the sprawling grounds in the rolling country-side often served as the perfect welcome to visitors. It was also secluded which served as a form of security form prying eyes.

Ellen and Hans were occupying one of the many living rooms on this evening, the same one that Hans had bought Ellen to during their first encounter. A fire was crackling in the grand fireplace again, casting warmth and soft light on everything that it could touch. With such an intense mentoring session from Claudia that morning, Hans allowed Ellen to have the afternoon off to do whatever she liked. They were now head-to-head in an intense game of chess, their backs arched over an ancient set made of bone which sparkled in the dim light. Hans was winning, but not by much. Their defeated pieces lined the sides of the board like spectators watching onwards at their peers. Intense silence filled the room; silence that was so intense you could almost feel it. The only thing that could be heard was the quiet crackling of the fire. Ellen made a move, a wide grin spreading over Hans' face.

"You shouldn't have," he chuckled. "Check mate."

Ellen sat back in the chair she had occupied those nights ago, folded her arms and pouted. "Every. Single. Time."

Hans slid back in his own chair and took a glass into his hand, swirling the contents. It had been established that he had a taste for aged whisky, and the specific one he had opened tonight was one given to him a number of decades ago from a Master in another clan. Ellen had since learned that clans were separate groups of Tempusmancers around the world, each clan belonging to a different country and occasionally, regions in those countries. She had also learned that the title 'Master' was only given to those that lead one of these clans and that they had the duty to look after their respective groups in times of need. Hans' specific clan consisted of well-functioning and intelligent Tempusmancers that could think for themselves and problem solve. Other Masters weren't as lucky, and had a high call-out and workload.

"You play quite well; so well, in fact, one would have a hard time guessing you've never played before."

Ellen smiled and then she remembered the voice that she had heard in the room earlier. Sire. Her eyebrows furrowed unintentionally as she recalled what the terrified man had said. Her mind was quick to whirl into thoughts, trying to join any links together. Nothing.

"Is everything okay, Ellen?" she heard Hans ask casually. He swirled the glass one more and emptied the remaining contents into mouth.

"Can I ask you something?"

Hans swallowed the whisky and placed the glass down. "Of course."

"What is a sire?"

Hans peered at her, his arms now nestled on his knees. "Why do you ask?"

"Because I heard someone say it today. I've only heard that word used with vampires but I don't know whether they exist..." Ellen explained.

Hans' eyes narrowed on her, his face hardening. "Oh, they exist. You'll hurt their feelings if they hear you say that they aren't real. We just don't have anything to do with them and they don't have anything to do with us. We operate in peace, letting each do their own. They stay out of our way and we return the favour. Did you see who said it by chance?"

She shook her head, no. "Whoever said it was behind a closed door. I only heard it as I was going to the dining room."

Hans abruptly stood up, grasped the glass he had put down and made his way to the mantle where several bottles were lined up. The various trinkets were still here, too, a space where the horse with the crouching man once was. The light from the fire in the fireplace danced across his face and shone in his eyes. He gazed into the flames. His back was to Ellen, so she couldn't see his facial emotions. His hair was held in a loose half-bun; the length of it folded half-way and looped into an elastic band. This was now tainted gold from the light hue.

"A sire," he began, his tone slow and purposeful. "Is a word the Necromancers use to describe their leader, their supreme ruler. The structure of that race isn't like ours – not one bit." He turned to face Ellen, her face was in a grimace now. "They were once a very reputable race and upheld morals that we still hold. All of those moral pillars were abolished when one of them in particular had a different ideology and overthrew the leader. When this happened, the hierarchy changed too. The sire stands above everyone else and keeps everyone else supressed. The word is somewhat shunned here. They believe that Necromancers should be thankful to serve their sire and if they aren't thankful, they receive punishment which is usually death. If you displease them, he will usually punish you indirectly by killing someone close to you. He also isn't afraid to dispense of his own for personal gain. One more; one less. It is nothing to him. It's nothing to Lucien." Hans spat his name.

Ellen bowed her head, trying to put the pieces of everything together. The more she did this, the more her heart sunk. Her nails sunk into the armrests of the chair. She wish she knew this, she could have told Hans and Claudia there and then. He could have been questioned. Hans pressed onwards.

"Lucien is hungry for one thing – power. Both Necromancers and Tempusmancers believe in a prophecy and it states that a person is born every century that is more powerful than all others. Knowing this, the sire has made it his vision to harness those abilities and create the hybrid I told you about earlier."

She felt a stone in her throat. Trying to speak, she stammered on her own words. Hearing all this made her feel as if she needed to faint; the light-headedness and nausea. She felt unnaturally warm and clammy, sweating starting to sit on her skin.

"We believe you're that person Ellen, and that they are trying to snatch you for experimental purposes. They were almost successful once already. It's important you remain safe. The fact you heard someone even mutter that word – yet alone, call someone that word – means that there is someone between us that is feeding off information to him. It also means that you were right, we can't trust anyone. It means we are compromised."

The atmosphere grew to be tense once more as there was an ashen silence. Hans lifted the glass to his lips and had a swig whilst Ellen sat in the armchair, lost for words. "You saved my life...," she stammered.

"It's part of a Master's duty. But I also think Claudia needs to hear this for herself so she can make an informed decision on how best to approach this. Will you call her or will I?" How Hans had brushed this off caught Ellen by surprise. He made it appear as if it was no big deal, just a simple feat. She felt herself further consumed by the nausea that had washed over her before. She felt as if she was flying high and then suddenly shot out of the sky. The happiness, the calmness, she experienced only ten minutes previously now dissipated.

"I will," she whispered, attempting to muster enough energy as she could. Given her current state, she didn't know whether she was strong enough to send the call out so it would reach Claudia. Regardless and determined to try, she closed her eyes and imagined Claudia in her mind. She called out to her, unsure whether she heard her. She called again, and again; energy draining from her body each and every time. Seconds ticked by, reaching a full minute. Nothing, not a sign. Feeling disappointed, she let herself slide further in her chair and bit her lip.

Nothing felt worse than defeat.

I will be there soon, she faintly heard someone say; a female. Claudia. She had heard Ellen after all. Those words were music to her ears and she felt a pinch of happiness return inside her.

"She's coming," she told Hans in relief. He nodded and smiled back at her warmly, instilling hope back into her. There was a quiet knock on the door before it opened and Claudia swept into the room with an aura of irritability around her. She carried a large, displeased look and her chest was raised tall and proud. She carried herself much differently to this morning; she looked much more disciplinary.

Hans raised his hand slightly to Ellen – don't say anything – which she caught from the corner of her eye. "Is everything okay?" he asked instead, raising an eyebrow.

"I just spent an hour and a half dealing with that pig Dvorak!" she exclaimed, obviously emotionally charged – a mix of frustration and anger. She spied the drink in Hans' hand. "I swear I could do with one of those right now."

Hans complied and poured her a glass, tapping it as he handed it to her waiting hand. He then ushered her into the second armchair.

"80 years old, this one. I take it Dvorak is still rather unhappy about the outcome of the meeting then?"

"Oh, very much so. He's started the blackmailing game already, threatening me that he will turn his clan to be dysfunctional and exposing themselves to the mortal populace. Can you believe his nerve? Can you? He's putting us at risk of being discovered even further than Hiddlestone!" The name of the writer rang in her ears and she remembered the disgust Hans showed towards him.

"Well Claudia. I think that's the second problem right now. We've found another one. A rather big one, at that."

Claudia's eyebrows shot upwards, forming large peaked arches over her eyes. "And what would that be?" Her voice was short, sharp, dreading.

"I think Ellen would be best to describe it to you. But we have a sneak." For the next five minutes, Ellen recounted what she had heard in the room. The unrecognisable high-pitch; the fear and weakness that filled the words. She described it a series of times prior to Claudia falling silent and calculating the situation.

"It's obvious the man and Lucien were conversing but it's a shame we didn't hear more. It sounds almost as if they are preparing something. An attack?" Her empty hand was near her lips now, her fingers resting on the delicate skin.

Hans nodded. "Only hearing those words, I would dare say that is exactly it. It's too plausible. How though, has got me stumped. They can't do anything inside of here. Even they know that." Ellen felt useless as, invisible, as she didn't know what to say in this conversation.

She didn't know enough about this life yet to be able to contribute anything of value.

"Do you think it's Dvorak? He seemed certain of..." Hans stopped talking, his words falling away. Ellen sensed that the Grand Master knew what he was alluding too thus, removing the need to finish the sentence.

"Well, who else could it be? No one else was as vocal as he was. You saw it with your own eyes!" Claudia finished off the drink and slid the glass onto the table, wiping her lips with a sleeve of her robe. "Should we pay him a visit? He is due to leave tomorrow morning back to his clan. I think it's best if Ellen comes with us."

The three of them left the room, Ellen lagging behind as she struggled to keep up with their large steps and quick pace. They snaked through several hallways, up a flight of stairs and a few hallways more. Finally, they rapped on the door or a room within the residential wing of the manor. The light-coloured wooden door opening, exposing the short and stumpy man. His face was a livid crimson once again, from the match with Claudia.

"'ello? Oh, it's you," he scoffed when he saw them. "You even bought her with you. How nice." Sarcasm oozed in his words and Ellen found herself quickly disliking this man.

"You didn't tell us you had non-physical company Dvorak!" Claudia said shrilly, pointing a finger at him.

"What are you talking about?" he asked, shaking his head. His mouth dropped open, as if to protest the accusation. The veins in his face were throbbing once again, the thin lines pulsing. "What company?"

"A certain sire?"

"You're off your rocker, woman! Why would I have ties to 'im?" He took a step backwards, away from the enraged Claudia. Fear spread over his face, his voice faltering.

"Dvorak. If it was up to you, Ellen would be on the street and probably dead by now by the man you worship!" Claudia made a threatening step towards him, towering over the cowering man. All of a sudden, the totem in Ellen's bedroom became real. Claudia was the rearing horse and Dvorak was the coward.

"But I didn't do anything you insane excuse of a Grand Master! My children were killed by that piece of work because I was against him!" He tripped over his own footing, and fell onto the floor. He was taking quick breaths now, quick and shallow.

"All the more excuse for you to be on his side! He told you to do this or to perish also! Isn't that right? Isn't that right?"

Even as a witness to this, Ellen was afraid of the woman who was now throwing words, sinking sharp daggers, into this man. The man was babbling incoherent words, overwhelmed. He rubbed his head.

"I've had enough. I revoke your Master-ship to your clan, and you will now be confined to this room until a relevant hearing can be organised."

Oblivious to her surroundings and consumed by what had unfolded, Ellen hadn't realised that several others had now surrounded them. They didn't appear normal however, dressed in metal armour that had similarities to that worn during the medieval period. Their faces were masked by a black piece of cloth that covered their nose, downwards. One of them dragged the man by the arms further into the room, left the room and slung shut the door. A heavy lock was put into place, and the guards left as silently as they had come.

Hans bent towards Ellen, whispering in her ear. "I am so sorry you had to see that." He saw Ellen gazing at the lock and added, "It's special, that lock. Only guards can remove it. It's guard-bound, you see. They're joined together through their souls, a bit like an imprint."

Claudia's face fell into despair, disappointment brewing within herself. Silently, she turned on her heel and wondered down the hallway. Her arms hung limply as she walked, the hem of the robe dragging on the floor rather than floating from the flow of the air. The ambience was heavy around them. Hans dropped a hand weightlessly onto and steered her in the opposite direction, neither of them uttering even the faintest peep.

Chapter Ten

Ellen's eyes scanned the courtroom, taking in its marvel and beauty. The room itself was cavernous with tall, sweeping ceilings made of rock and wooden beams. The walls were similar, predominantly stone that was bracketed by dark wood, and the floor itself was made of highly-polished marble. As the room was underground, it was also cool and occasionally made Ellen shiver and the hairs on her skin stand on end. A marvellous, intricately detailed gold chandelier that was drilled into the ceiling hung at the forward of the room, bathing everything under it in a pale-yellow light. Two long, bench-like tables stretched from one wall to the other; the second elevated on a platform so that the observers in the gallery. Seated behind them were eighteen members of the Committee; eighteen which was usually twenty. But not today. One of their own members was being tried, and Claudia was yet to enter as per procedure. A small table was set up to the side to accommodate a scribe who was now busying herself unwinding a scroll.

The gallery was full of spectators whispering amongst each other; the masses usually only arriving in force when someone of prominence was being tried or whether it involved Necromancers. It was like the squeaking of mice, so quiet but together as one, so loud. Ellen found herself on the front bench in an optimal viewing position, tightly nestled between Guardian Rolland and someone who she had never seen before. Flaming red hair, dark as night skin and a heavy accent told Ellen that she wasn't local to this region. Hans had fought hard prior to the trial, banning her from attending but Claudia had insisted otherwise and saw it as beneficial. The final result was that she would be able to attend but only in the company of Rolland. At times she felt as if she was being babysat but in reality, she was only young in this world and needed guidance and experience. Being better than nothing, she accepted and was now waiting eagerly on the bench-seats with everyone else for the trial to begin.

Rolland had taken it on himself to educate her about the legal process, and was giving her a whispering commentary in her ear about what to expect and etiquette customs that needed to be observed. He also pointed to the Grand Committee members, giving a brief yet intimate description of each person. The members were diverse, coming from all corners of the globes, as were their features. Skin shades ranged from ghastly white to a rich, chocolate brown; hair, bald to floor length and white to black, faces were shaped from pointed to well-rounded. They all wore the same ceremonial robes of pale gold, a symbol of honourable status and were expressionless. Her eyes rested on Hans who was seated in the middle-front, left of the chair that Claudia would be occupying shortly. His face was neutral, both hands entwined and resting on the table in front of him. He also refused to make eye contact with anyone, rather intensely focusing on the edge of the table in front of him.

There was a sudden bang! - similar to an explosion - and heads in the gallery turned rapidly towards the entrance doors. The heavy panels of wood flew open and a group of guards marched inwards along the aisle. Ellen could just make out the small man, Dvorak, amongst them, dwarfed by the others. The metal armour they wore clanged with each and every step, the metallic sound bouncing and echoing off the walls. Once at the top of the aisle and facing towards the Grand Committee, the front guards broke from the line and retreated, followed by the guards that were on the sides of Dvorak. Those that stood behind the man remained there, ensuring that he couldn't escape if he tried; although, Ellen had the inkling that the guards wouldn't need to be there physically to be able to stop him. An aura was given off by them, an aura filled with power and might.

All eyes were on Dvorak now who stood defiantly at the front, his eyes transfixed on the empty seat; so transfixed that he may have gone cross-eyed. There were still a few stolen whispers in the gallery, a mix of curiosity and accusatory. It was difficult to make out what these individual whispers were but that didn't bother Ellen. Rumours had leaked of what had happened in the meeting that day and most had a very heavily weighted opinion. It seemed clear that he wasn't, by any means, a popular Tempusmancer yet alone a Master. Ellen suspected the only ones that supported him were from his very own clan, and even they seemed few and far between in the gallery.

The scribe rose from her seat and cleared her throat. No one seemed to notice her; that was, until she boomed over them. This was very unexpected and several members jumped in their seats.

"Silence!" she shouted to the gallery. Her command was loud, and the room immediately fell silent under her piercing stare. The atmosphere went from being excited to being instantly electric. It was starting; the infamous trial was starting! And they would be here to witness it all unfold or, in Dvorak's case, unravel. Or at least, that's what everyone was expecting at this moment.

"All rise for Her Honor, the Grand Master!" The observers did as they were told, several removing head garments whilst standing up and bowing their heads. Ellen mimicked them, rising from her chair and training her gaze onto the stone floor; Rolland brushing against her as he did the same. It was considered impolite to watch Claudia take her seat, and so eyes were often diverted downwards.

"You may sit," the scribe instructed once more. There was a brief flurry of movement as everyone retook their seats on the benches, the sound of bodies thumping on wood filling the room.

Silence shrouded the room once more, so quiet that you could easily hear the nib of the fountain pen scribbling on the scribes' parchment.

Ellen now looked at the completed Committee, Claudia's throat shifting as she cleared it. The strict woman looked through her glasses, down her nose at the man in front of her.

"Master Dvorak, you are summoned here today on suspicion of treason. How do you plead?"

"Not guilty, your Honor." The gallery broke out in hasty murmurs; murmurs that were quashed with the wave of a hand. Ellen observed some of the faces around her, all of which were flabbergasted. The Grand Committee remained poised and patient, thinking within themselves and disregarding the reactions of those around them. They couldn't let that influence their decisions. They were here to be impartial and deliver an unbiased judgement.

"In a previous meeting, you moved to stop protection of Miss Ellen Nightingale despite her having faced death by Necromancer. A short time later, a member of our group heard someone pleading with the sire to divert something to a later time. They were presumably in a communicative trance. How do you describe this?" Claudia's gaze into Dvorak was akin to her gazing into his soul. It was ruthless; calculating. She was prowling for the truth and nothing was going to stand in her way. There was a panic within the gallery as the word 'sire' was said. It was to be expected; it was a somewhat taboo word.

"To answer the first part of your recount," he started calmly. Everyone fell silent once more, comprehending each word as it was spoken. "Was that I was acting in the best interests of my clan which is part of my duty as a Master. I will not let any of them come to harm if I can help it, even if it means harming the skin on my own body. To answer the second part, that was not me. I do not affiliate myself with any of the Necromancers, let alone the self-professed 'sire'."

"Master Dvorak, the Grand Committee is aware that your children perished at the hands of the sire some years ago. What is there to say that he threatened to kill your spouse too unless you answered his calls? Did his bidding within this manor?" The questions from Claudia were pointed, sharp daggers into Dvorak's composure. There were several oooooh's and aaaaah's as audience members gasped at the thought. Serving Lucien was despicable evil, regarded to only be done by those with the most tainted souls.

His face fell, colour draining from his already-pale complexion. These presumptions were wild and extremely formidable.

"I assure you that I am against him and do not stand as one with his scum. My allegiance is with the Tempusmancers and Tempusmancers only. I swore that when I took the incantation as a Master."

Claudia lowered her glasses from the crook of her nose and folded them onto the table in front of her. She rubbed the pressure spot the nose-pieces left, unconsciously, and deep in deliberation. "I believe that the only away to determine the truth," she placed particular emphasis on the last word. Ellen saw Dvorak's legs shake slightly, his body swaying on the spot. His chest rose and dropped faintly but quickly. He knew what was about to hit him. "Is to administer a Seek."

Dvorak gave a curdling cry, Ellen watching as the man went from being defiant to weak and helpless. Despite not knowing what a Seek was, she could only assume it was something terrible as the gallery fell into shock around him. Mouths dropped open and shrieks erupted and there was commotion. It was disarray. Trying to get a handle of the situation, Claudia called for order. Her voice overpowered the room and everyone immediately settled.

"What's a Seek?" asked Ellen, leaning closer to Rolland. She wasn't sure if he had heard her but he responded soon after with a gentle whisper.

"A Seek is something that the guards do to determine what actually happened. Essentially, the guards access the persons mind and can see every memory they have in there, kind of like probing. They can see everything that person has done. There is no privacy, and it usually leaves them feeling exhausted and violated afterwards."

Ellen looked on in horror as the guards seized Dvorak by the arms and led him away, through a door to the side, and out of the onlooker's sight. He was kicking, he was digging his heels into the rocks, and she heard him scream in pained anguish. It demonstrated how truly brutal a Seek was. She hoped - she prayed - she wouldn't have to experience it in her lifetime.

And then the door he was lead through slammed closed and Dvorak's hysterical screaming became silence. That was the end of the public trial.

- - -

A very restless and frustrated Lucien slammed his fist onto the desk, the knock on wood by muscle, skin and bone being the only sound in the room. He was by himself, but he didn't mind. Lucien was his own best company and he spent many moments alone in his office. The darkness, the privacy. It was the birthplace of all his directions, his work and his leadership as well as his masterminded plans. Little did anyone know that he killed his teacher here, but that was his secret and his pride. It also held a special place in his cold heart.

He let out an impatient sigh and lay back in the chair, letting the back recline under his weight like his teacher did before him. He hated it when his plan didn't go accordingly but especially hated it when his contact didn't inform him like he was asked to. It had been a full day now without hearing from him, and he was growing tired. Did he have to begin executing the next step without receiving the insight? It was a leering possibility; a possibility that was now on his radar. Either way, the potential blood shed was music to his ears and very well welcomed.

He gripped his favourite letter opening knife from its holder and weaved it between his fingers.

In and out.

In and out.

The silver knife twinkled hauntingly in the dim light, the shiny blade reflecting his face. He looked unkempt, the stress he was experiencing wreaking havoc on his appearance. Since the infamous Hans Grey had rescued the girl, everything had fallen to the wayside and he had to rely on his leading hand to keep him informed. And now, it seemed that his leading hand had no longer regarded his bidding as priority. This would call for punishment. Unless... No, he would give his help another fifteen minutes. If by that time he received no word, then he would think of how to punish him.

He mentally replayed Plan B in his mind, down to minute-by-minute increments. All the key players were already on standby in case they got the call. In case they got his call. And then they would act immediately, striking on his command. He mused at the thought, the sight of success making him smile. Not too much longer. And this time, he would make sure the girl didn't get away.

"Sire," a weak voice called to him. "Can you hear me?" His heartbeat leapt to a quicker tempo. He didn't show this of course; he couldn't.

"I hope you can give me more information," he replied simply; mentally.

"They have administered the Seek, so we do not have much time. They are planning on doing an outing with the girl in the coming days - soon. The perfect time would be then."

These were the words that Lucien wanted to hear; the words he was so desperately itching to be told. And now that he was told them, he couldn't be happier. The rats were going into the rattrap and he would have that girl in his grasp again soon.

"Can you provide me with more specific information when it becomes available?"

"Yes, my Lord."

"Don't fail me," he cautioned. He knew it had the same effect as hanging a sword above his helps head.

And then the feeble voice was gone.

Lucien sat back upright and hefted the knife into the desk. It cut through the wood relatively easily, the blade being sharp and well maintained. It was now stuck in the wood, swaying back and forth like it was made of rubber. It was only a matter of time before the Tempusmancers would be kneeling before him, swaying on their knees begging for their lives.

Begging for their lives like his teacher.

He let out a hearty laugh, arising from deep within his chest. Soon.

Chapter Eleven

It was a dark and gloomy day.

A storm had descended upon the manor, the sky consisting of deep, deep grey clouds with patches of purple that stretched as far over the horizon as one could see. The heavens had opened and it was now dumping a deluge of rain. The grounds of the property were sodden and puddles were accumulating wherever they could, some almost worthy enough of being a splash-pool. The giant wet had resulted in the groundskeepers being called off-duty for the time being but this didn't worry them.

It never did.

A steady, cascading waterfall came from the eaves of the buildings, all of which were beyond capacity and were overflowing. It would provide for a good shower if soap or body wash was on hand. One would only need to spend five seconds outside to become equally as drenched as the grass beneath their feet.

Ellen sat in the window seat of her room, her eyes following each of the dotted trails the raindrops left behind as they hit the glass and slithered downwards. It was a mind-numbing thing to do, although thoroughly relaxing. When she wasn't busy, relaxing here was one of her favourite things to do.

She was alone, again, the newfound freedom overwhelming as she was so used to being in Hans or Claudia's company. She wasn't quite sure what to do with all this free time. Each of their days, from the wee hours of the morning to the late hours of the evening, were devoted to the proceedings of the Dvorak trial which had continued behind closed doors. She knew nothing as the Grand Committee weren't allowed to discuss it. It had been three days since it had resumed; three days of loneliness.

She had tried approaching others in the hallways, the library and the dining room but they were quick to carry off as if they suddenly remembered they had an urgent appointment to attend. If she wasn't light-hearted, she would have taken offense to their sudden departure but it was humorous to see the excuses they developed on their feet and their panicked faces. One even went as far to say she had a meeting with Claudia during the time which Ellen and everyone else knew she was in the trial. Deep down, Ellen had the inkling that it was only because she was viewed as trouble; they feared they would be attacked if they associated themselves with her.

Now, she found herself staring out of the window, her mind drifting to the turn of events that her life had taken. She then started having flashbacks of her childhood, her parents always happy and supporting her with whatever she chose to do. She remembered the first time she rode a bicycle, the first time she made a cake, the first time she won an academic award in high school. A tear rolled down her cheek; rolling down like the raindrops on the other side of the window.

She missed them.

And she missed them dearly.

She felt her chest heave and fall; again, heave and fall. She took a fistful of the soft, fleece blanket she wrapped herself in and held it up to her eyes as she began to sob. The fleece was quick to soak her tears. She leaned the back of her head on the wall of the window seat and started to take several deep breaths.

Everything will be okay.

She saw her own reflection on the window, her hair tucked into an unkempt bun and her eyes shiny. She retrained her focus and stared at the wet scenery around her. The world was feeling her pain.

There was a knock on the door, and she snapped her head towards it. She wasn't expecting a visitor. Rolland had poked his head through a small gap and now looked at her with wide eyes.

"I heard someone sobbing on my way to grab something to eat. Are you okay?" he asked, spying her depressed state.

Ellen nodded, wiping her face once more with the blanket.

"You know Ellen. We might be classified as immortal but we are still human and experience a broad range of emotions. No one can take that away from us. It is okay to feel these and to ask for help when we need it. It's hard but it's something that can help."

She felt herself break down and her head rolled into her hands. Rolland slid into the room and closed the door behind him. He walked over to her and patted her back, trying to comfort her like his parents comforted him when he was a child. She broke down further but then found the strength to compose herself a bit more. Satisfied, Rolland sat opposite her on the window seat and balanced one of his hands on his knee.

"Did I tell you," he said, softly. His voice was understanding, calming and soothing. It eased the burden off Ellen slightly. "That I lost my parents, too, when I was young?"

Ellen, in response, shook her head. He didn't tell her that. In actuality, he hadn't told her much about himself at all.

"Oh yes. They perished in one of the Necromancer purges. They were given the option – to become one of them or to suffer at their hands. Like all noble Tempusmancers, they refused and so they suffered. My father was dispensed off immediately, in front of mother. Mother was kept as a slave girl and entertainment until one of Lucien's hands grew tired of her and killed her too. I somehow managed to escape. The Grand Committee was alerted of my situation and so – when I was of age – I gained specialist training in being Guardian. And now here I am."

Ellen watched Rolland as he spoke. His usual perfectly straight posture sagged, and his fingers tapped against his leg. It was clear he was reliving the moment as he recounted the story. His voice faltered ever-so-lightly and he blinked more than usual. Was he blinking back tears? They both shared the moment together before a question popped into Ellen's mind.

"What is the role of a Guardian?" she asked out of interest. But she also wanted to change the subject to something more airy. She wasn't quite aware of what it entailed and the more she learnt about this world, the more she became fascinated.

"A Guardian looks out for others in his clan and monitors their wellbeing. We are also amongst the first to investigate if something minor has gone astray; you know, like a disturbance of some kind. It could be that a mortal has a suspicion that we exist or if we have vanished in front of them. The fact that I work part time as a police officer in the mortal realm is somewhat of an inside joke between the Tempusmancers. But it also helps me in covering our tracks if I need to."

A light-bulb went off in the back of her mind, like it must have gone off for Edison when he was inventing. An epiphany; an epiphany that she was proud of.

"Is that why you were there that day? When the Necromancer was chasing me?" She had a million and one questions, and couldn't blurt them out fast enough. "You were there to control the situation, weren't you? You were diverting the services to believe that nothing paranormal occurred? You were protecting the secret that we exist?"

Rolland smiled, lifting up a finger as if it was a gun and playfully flicking it upwards. Spot on. "Hans was right. You are very quick indeed. And that's correct."

"Do you go to many?"

"Only ones that are on my shift and within this clans' territory. On that note, I was getting ready to investigate a small disturbance in Havenlock City if you wanted to join? Both Hans and Claudia are happy for me to take you with me. You can see how it's done and if you get the taste for it, you can always apply for specialist training when you are the right age."

Ellen opened her mouth, ready to argue with Rolland. But Hans had said she was of age? He held up a finger, a reaction to put an end to an imminent protest. Without a doubt, he had heard all of this before. "Tempusmancers are only eligible for specialist roles once they have been converted for at least three years. You need to have a really good grasp on your abilities before you can be assigned a specific role. And even then, they only accept those that are the most promising."

"So, it's kind of like a university admission then? You need to a good enough score to be accepted?"

"It's just like university, to the point that it does take a while to achieve full specialisation too. Even then, you never quite know everything." He winked, and rose to his feet from the window seat. "Care to join?" He straightened his clothes, and smoothed back his hair with a palm.

"Sure," she replied, her interest piqued. She was looking forward to the experience, but more importantly she hoped it would take her mind off things; things like her parents, Lucien, and the ordeal of being snatched.

"In that case, I need to finish making preparations before we leave. I'll come grab you, in say... fifteen minutes?"

"Sure."

Rolland grabbed her shoulder and gave it a gentle, warm squeeze before he left. She then strode to the wardrobe in the corner of her room and changed into something more suitable and presentable to the public. This also involved brushing her hair to make it neater, and less caveman or jungle-like.

   I'll be okay after all, she thought, smiling to herself in the mirror.

Chapter Twelve

The village district of Havenlock City was bustling with early-morning foot traffic. Professionals were traversing the streets like ants, holding steaming paper cups of coffee – delicious goodness and often revered liquid gold; students were walking in herds, laughing at jokes or dragging the balls of their feet on the floor and cursing parents for forcing them to go; and, seniors were deep in discussions with their friends over tea and a devilish slice of cake. They picked the soft sponge apart, jab by jab with the prongs of their dessert forks. The village itself was tidy and held significance to the region, the history captured largely within the historic buildings that lined the streets and in historians that took great care of their community. Due to the narrow distance between them, the streets were closed to vehicular traffic which added to the village feel that this district was renowned for.

Ellen and Rolland had arrived not five minutes ago, and were already seated at one of the many cafes. This one seemed to be popular with the locals as most of the tables were filled, and there was friendliness in the air. It had a coffeehouse feel to it, warm hues on the walls which were decorated with prints of a fictional newspaper, comfortable wrap-around chairs and benches, and the smell of roasting caffeine in the air. Despite the friendly atmosphere inside, the pair opted to sit outside where there were less people and the breeze could gently buffet around them.

He was giving her a quiet briefing of the situation at hand, using a hushed voice so those around them couldn't overhear them: a Tempusmancer had attempted to vanish in haste and had managed to splice off an arm and a leg. Before he had the time to correct himself, an elderly concerned citizen stumbled upon the floating body parts and quickly alerted authorities. She, herself, was in disbelief however, she convinced them anyway to have a look and at least listen to what she had to say. The culprit is already long gone but damage control still had to be done.

"And that's where I step in," Rolland told Ellen, pointing both of his pointer fingers to himself and giving a smile. "I'm the plain-clothes officer that will convince her that it was just a figment of her imagination. And she will believe me because that's the way I will direct things, if you know what I mean." He gave her a wink as if it was an inside joke.

A very lame inside joke at that.

The young, brown haired and blue eyed waitress that took their orders now arrived at the table, placing two plain white, steaming porcelain mugs in front of them. She immediately turned so she was facing Rolland, her back to Ellen. She was obviously interested in him. She tried hard, so hard that it oozed from her.

The hair playing.

The straightening of her shirt.

The battering of eyelids.

"Would you like anything else today?" she asked, flicking her hair behind her. Her voice was sickly sweet, forced and unnatural. It made Ellen sick, and it looked like it had that effect on Rolland too.

"No, thank-you," he replied emotionlessly, ignoring the waitress and refusing to look at her. Ellen didn't blame him. She let out a small chuckle but it wasn't silent enough. The waitress threw a scowl in her direction and trudged back into the shop, behind the counter where one of her colleagues was waiting. As if on cue, both of them turned to look at Rolland, completely disregarding that he was in the company of Ellen. The look on their faces – want, need, lust – was enough.

"How far away was the accident?" she asked, diverting her attention form the the waitresses and taking a sip from the tea she ordered. It was sweet, fruity, and fragrant. Just the way she liked it. The hot liquid warmed her insides; warmed her soul. It also calmed her nerves. She wasn't sure what to expect from today.

"Two blocks away. I just need you to promise me one thing..." His eyes flickered to hers and then down to the mug that was in his hands. It seemed like his promise would be something major; something drastic.

"Yes?" she asked, curiously. She held her breath, readying for what was to come.

"Whatever you do, do not use your abilities. This is pretty serious business and we can't afford to escalate things by making a mistake here."

Ellen nodded, understanding the situation. Her worry dissipated as quickly as it had come. Hans had described this many a times to her, telling her to restrict using her abilities unless she was with him or he had given her the all clear after enough training. She respected this, she knew she had a long way to go just yet. She wasn't about to break this promise whilst she was with Rolland and after seeing the opening of the trial of Dvorak, she knew straying from Hans' rules and playing up wasn't worth it.

The memories of the shrieking man were still fresh in her mind.

The pair sat in silence for a while longer as they finished off their drinks, Rolland wiping his lips as the last of the coffee filtered from the cup and down his throat. Together, they stood from the table and slowly made their way through the stoned streets of the village centre, the breeze now chilling their cheeks. Every so often, Rolland would point out a heritage building and describe the history behind it, Ellen hanging onto each and every word. He had a remarkable and alluring story-telling ability, drawing from both memory and learned knowledge.

They stopped before a cobble-stoned walkway intersection, Rolland now turning to Ellen. "It happened in the park just across the intersection there."

Ellen glanced across where there was a small park. It had an abundance of greenery, and created a serene and tranquil place. Large, ancient trees were dotted along a winding pathway and trimmed, landscaped lawns sprawled across as far as it could reach. Birds chirped in the trees, a somewhat postcard perfect setting. There were a few families enjoying the outdoors as well as individuals doing their usual yoga routines. But one of them stood out like sore thumb.

An elderly lady stood alone in the shade of a tree, her arms around her torso as if she was holding herself. A light, beige coloured headscarf was draped over her hair, and a matching shawl was draper around her shoulders. She was clutching a weaved handbag close to herself, clutching so tight that the blood in her hands had stopped circulating and they were a pale, ill-looking white. Every so often, she took a quick glance at her surroundings before returning her stare to the floor.

"I'll need you to do something so she doesn't put us together," Rolland told Ellen, emphasising the end of the sentence. "Take a stroll around the park of a nap on the bench; it's up to you but don't make it seem obvious that you know."

Ellen nodded and entered the park first. She found an empty bench, outstretched her arms and portrayed herself as someone who came here for a mid-morning nap. Now that she was in position, she watched as Rolland strolled through the park and approached the elderly woman. They shook hands, and launched into an animated discussion. Judging by the hand movements, Ellen assumed that she was now recounting what she saw. Rolland pulled out a notepad and jotted notes as she spoke, his pen skipping from one edge of the page to the other. The woman now had a grin on her face, brimming from ear to ear. He pocketed the notepad and shook hands, watching her as she left the park.

And then there was a sudden barrage of screaming.

Women, children, and men ran out of the park, their hands at their mouths, fleeing as fast as they could. Children were picked up and had their eyes covered by the hands of their guardians.

It was a state of disarray, disarray that Ellen had once seen before. She was suddenly pulled out of the semi-conscious trance state she was in by the commotion that surrounded her. What was once a peaceful park turned into a field of terror.

She shot up to her feet, and scanned the park hastily. What caused this? What happened?

Her eyes took in everything around her, and then she did a double take.

A man was lying on the pathway – less than hundred metres from Ellen - with his eyes closed and a hand grabbing at his chest. A crimson pool was forming around his torso, the liquid also staining the singlet and cargo shorts he was wearing. The blood pool was getting bigger, and it was getting bigger fast. The few onlookers that could tolerate the sight of it were now flocking to him. A middle-aged man tore off the shirt he was wearing and pushed down, acting like a clot to the wound. Another grabbed the man's wrist and searched tirelessly for a pulse. His face was growing grimmer by the minute.

"Someone call an ambulance!" he yelled to the bystanders.

Ellen felt a hand twist around her upper-arm and tug her away from the scene. The grip cut into her skin, it hurt.

"What did you do?" she heard Rolland snarl into her ear.

"Nothing, honest!" she replied. She took a look at Rolland, his lips in a tight line and his face red and livid.

"Ellen, things like that don't just happen." He pulled her so that she was now facing him. "Find an empty place, vanish, and go back to the manor. I will follow shortly once I get to the bottom of this. Don't think that you're getting away from this. It really is something to take a human life."

Ellen opened her mouth to argue but it was to no avail. She felt tears brim in her eyes, her heart pounding loudly yet missing beats.

"That's an order!" he barked. He then gave Ellen a final glare and retraced his steps back to the scene.

She surged through the park and exited, traversing the many walkways until she finally found an empty, barren street. She fell to her knees, not sure of what to think.

Did she really do it?

Was it all her doing?

"I can't return. I can't let Hans down anymore."

She pondered on her next move, where she should go. Fumbling to her feet, she imagined the location and painted it in her mind the best she could. She glanced around her to make sure no one was watching, closed her eyes, and took a sprinting step.

The next thing she felt was her body become weightless.

And then it hit the solid ground beneath her.

Chapter Thirteen

Ellen felt her body become weightless as if she was lighter than a feather. She drifted in nothingness for a split second; suspended in between destinations, and in a state of limbo.

And then her feet hit solid ground and she came back to reality.

She opened her eyes and was met with a familiar site, a site that stirred a mix of emotions within her. Sadness, anger, and loneliness. They all reared their ugly heads.

Ellen's childhood home loomed over her, the painted-white manor bringing back a surge of memories. The once well-groomed flower beds were a sickly brown and had begun welting; the gravel driveway was being invaded by weeds, and the lawns that she once played on as a child had started shooting upwards. It was becoming derelict but with her parents perished, she wasn't quite confident of its impending fate.

Was it hers? Could she come back to live here?

It was a possibility. As far as she fathomed, she was the only child and therefore the sole beneficiary of her parent's belongings.

She moved forwards – towards the building – one step at a time. Each step placed her one step closer; each step seeded and bloomed emotions which brewed like a wild storm. She perched onto one of the steps, and then the other, and the other. Her feet were as heavy as gold bars, weighing her down as she approached the front door. Each time she placed one of her feet down, there was a knock on the wooden slats. They almost sounded as if they were trying to warn her; it's a trap, escape whilst you can. It seemed like an eternity had passed by the time she reached for the metal handle, and laid one finger on it. But then she drew her hand back, overwhelmed.

The handle was searing hot and scolded her finger. It glowed red, the same shade of angry red that were glowing embers. Ellen hastily moved backwards, almost tripping over her own feet. She blinked, and the redness was gone.

"I can do this," she told herself. "It's just your imagination."

She let a fresh spell of air fill her lungs and pushed down on the handle. The door slowly opened, exposing the lifeless, cold hallway which used to be warm and welcoming. She stepped across the threshold, onto the rug that her mother had put there years ago to catch dirt and other unwanted debris. Her mouth opened by habit, to call out she was home but then she realised that no one was here and it was caught in her throat, a giant lump that sat there stubbornly.

With the hardest part over, Ellen walked to the doorway that marked the entry of the lounge room and gazed inside reminiscently. Someone had already been here.

The chair and sofa was covered in stiff storage plastic, as was the coffee table and the antiques cabinet. A fine layer of dust had already began accumulating on the coverings, meaning that it must have been done a time go. The TV was disconnected from the power outlet and that, too, was flicked off at the wall.

She wandered into the kitchen.

Someone had done the job consistently – plastic coverings and electrical appliances unplugged.

Letting this mull over her mind, she doubled out of the kitchen and vaulted up the staircase. Both, her own bedroom door and her parents' were ajar but only just. She caught a small glimpse of the inside of the rooms, and made to go to hers first. And then she stopped in her tracks.

She traced back her steps and visited her parent's room. Not knowing what to expect - what was waiting for her behind closed doors - she held her breath and pushed on the door. It slowly swung open, revealing a bedroom that had been meticulously cleaned from top to bottom. The bed was cleanly made and sheets looked freshly laundered and showed no signs of death. Or murder. Her vision became blurry and Ellen found this the perfect time to move on. She closed the door, hoping – needing - that shutting it would give her renewed strength and determination to carry on forwards.

She turned from the panel of wood that now lay between her and her parents' private belongings – from the room they nursed her in as a baby – and wandered to her own. She placed her palm on the handle and swung it open. Her room, too, had been cleaned. Taking a few hesitant baby-steps into the space she had occupied for years, she cast her eyes in each direction. Everything was back in its respective place and the library book was nowhere to be seen.

She pulled the chair from behind her desk and sat down like many a time she had before; before, when her life was normal.

When her parents were still alive and killing someone was unimaginable.

When she wasn't a murderer. A murderer like Lucien.

She stared up at the ceiling, wandering, her mind drifting and unconsciously looking for a sign that everything will be okay. A glint of light caught her attention and her gaze sat transfixed on the small object in front of her. She picked it up and let it fumble in her shaking hands. The totem was still there and it reminded Ellen that everything was reality. It had all happened. It continued shining in her palm, reflecting the rays on sunlight that entered through her bedroom window.

"I wouldn't have taken you to be one that resigns so easily, my child," a whisper came from behind her; soft, authoritative yet motherly. A hand fell on Ellen's shoulder and she was tempted to shrug it off. But something told her to resist.

"I'm not who everyone thinks I am. I can't live up to the light everyone holds me to," she uttered. Each word was difficult; each word came from deep down. Her eyes connected with Claudia's and Ellen's heart fell heavy with disappointment.

"What do you think happened?" the Grand Master asked her. Ellen was searching for the anger; the threat of in her voice of an upcoming trial. Surely there were guards waiting outside to escort her.

"I killed someone. It's fairly obvious, even Rolland said so." She was now growing hysterical and her words were wavering. She hated how composed Claudia was in front her.

"Guardian Rolland thought that. But did you make it happen? Was it in your mind?"

"Well, no... But he's had years of experience an-"

Claudia spoke, cutting of Ellen's words. "Even the greatest of our kind make mistakes, and he was quick to judge without first properly analysing facts. Unfortunately, he can also have quite a temper especially when he is out on duty. What you need to understand is," she paused and took Ellen's hands in hers, the totem now in both of their palms. "That no one is perfect. And if that doesn't make you feel any better, then remember that he doesn't have the power to do anything to you. Those types of formalities are mine and Hans'."

Ellen let out a giant gust of a sigh.

"But what if I did it?"

"You didn't. Do you remember what you need to do? You need to consciously have that in your mind. Things like that don't just happen."

"What if I was thinking about it?"

"You'd remember, no doubt."

"But-"

"Ellen. It was a set up. Generally, things this ummm...," Claudia swirled her empty hand in the air, trying to grasp for invisible words. "Messy are done by rogues or Necromancers. Not by innocent people such as yourself. To the point – you didn't do it."

"Dvorak is in trial though, he couldn't possibly be there!"

Claudia let go of Ellen's hand and let her own hands smooth over Ellen's hair. "The trial proceedings are private but there can always be more than one traitor. They want to make you vulnerable. Don't let them do that. We can only help you so much but if you vanish off to random places, we can't even do that much. It's all you."

Ellen sat in her chair, the words cutting into her and etching themselves into her mind.

She was foolish, again. She exposed herself; exposed herself more than she should have. She was snatched already and she didn't want to relive that experience.

Claudia clapped her shoulder. "I believe Hans is waiting downstairs. Let's not keep him any longer than we need to."

Together, they left the bedroom in silence. Just as Ellen was about to stop and glance backwards, Claudia leaned down to her ear and told her: "do not look back. It makes it harder. Leave what has happened behind and move forward. You can't move into the future if you remember your past in the present." Ellen knew she was correct and they filed down the stairs.

Hans came into view as they descended, more and more of him becoming exposed with each step down they took. First his shoes, followed by the bottom of his pants and then his t-shirt. Finally, Ellen saw his face. His hands were behind his back and his face portrayed absolutely no emotion. He was stiff as a board as he watched the two women go towards him.

Ellen rubbed the totem that was still in her palm, as if for luck. Feeling tearful she approached Hans, trying hard not to think of what he was thinking about her.

But this wasn't needed.

Hans held out both of his arms and Ellen walked into them. The embrace was comforting, and he was all she had close to a father figure. She needed him and it became more obvious than it ever had been. It was a tender moment, one that Claudia refused to interrupt. No words were spoken but no words were needed. Claudia ran a hand through Ellen's hair gently. And then the embrace of Hans and Ellen broke as Claudia cleared her throat.

"Should we move on?"

"Let's," Hans replied, an arm lingering on Ellen's back. Claudia stood on the other side of Ellen, so now she was in between the two Masters. Claudia's arm, too, rested on the young girls back.

"Together. On the count of three. One. Two," she counted. "Three".

And the trio vanished.

They vanished as a team, and as one.

Chapter Fourteen

"And then what happened?"

"Mortals started running, panicked. I then identified the source of the commotion and that's when I saw Ellen on her feet, staring at the dying man that was lying on the pathway a short distance away."

There was silence – a pause – as those within the room took the information in.

"And what did you say to her after that?"

"I implied that she killed the mortal. I then commanded her to come back to the manor, and that I would be speaking to her Master about this."

"I don't know how many times we need to keep reminding you Guardian Rolland that you need to control your temper and emotions. There is no denying that you are exemplar in your role and almost born into it, but if you can't control your anger and your accusations then we will have no other choice. You understand this, don't you?"

"Yes, of course."

"Discharging you from the role is not something we would like to see happen however, it is a role of prestige and carries great responsibilities. Act accordingly Guardian Rolland, or you will see yourself relieved. You may leave."

Guardian Rolland spun on his toes and strode across the room, official robes swaying behind him. His lips were in a ruler-straight lin and his eyebrows were furrowed. Ellen watched as he gripped the door, and slid outside.

She was sitting beside Hans and Claudia in the boardroom. Hans was drumming his fingers on the table, appearing slightly uncomfortable that he had to witness a warning being issued to someone that he worked closely with. Claudia, on the other hand, rested a hand on an armrest and now supported her chin with two fingers, a tell-tale sign that she was caught between a rock and a hard place.

"I only wish we knew what they were up to," she finally sighed, sliding into the back of her chair and letting her back slump. Neither of them had to say who 'they' were; the trio knew very well who 'they' referred to.

"Lucien is unpredictable. Even if he had a plan, it would probably change on the whim. Everything is constantly changing with him. We know this. Even if we knew what they were thinking, it is difficult to prepare anything," Hans replied, trying to comfort the frustrated woman.

Claudia slammed her fist on the table in frustration, strands of her hair falling out of the loose bun that was on the nape of her neck. She knew Hans was right, and it wasn't worth trying to say otherwise. "I feel like I can't properly protect our people or to prepare them for what's to come. Do you know how bad that feels?"

She was anguished. It was a desperate time.

"I do," Hans replied simply. Of course he did. He was Grand Master too once and he had to deal with the Necromancer problems that came about during his reign.

Ellen shrunk back in her chair. She was not quite sure whether they were aware that she was still in the room or if they had completely forgotten of her existence. She pushed harder against the backing, as if hoping that it would absorb her into it. But it didn't and so she listened and waited patiently.

"Where do we take it from here?" Claudia continued. "Do we stay quiet or do we let everyone know that something is brewing and to be on alert? A call to arms so early would only spark hysteria in some, and that would cause a separate headache. Not to mention, if someone within these walls is providing intel to the others, they would immediately know and can counter us."

Hans weighed up the options and nodded in agreeance. "We need to keep it quiet, between us. From experience and teachings, Lucien seems very adverse when it comes to attacking. If history taught us anything, it is that he acts by himself and a small clan of what he deems to be his strongest men or men that he doesn't fear to sacrifice. He takes joy in undertaking the formalities himself, and likes to claim the most kills."

Claudia considered this for a moment, each word that Hans had spoken sounding accurate. "This does sound like it's the best way forward. And what do you think of this Ellen?"

A sense of shock rose within Ellen.

Not only did it seem that they knew she was there the entire time but now they were asking for input?

But she didn't have any experience whatsoever! What could she possibly contribute to the defence of Tempusmancers?

"I – I don't know," she stuttered, lost for words. She wanted to add something but she also wanted it to be worthwhile. "If it's anything that I've come to realise, it's that Lucien seems to thrive on other people's pain. I doubt he will let others take away the thing that he thrives on."

It seemed to be the best she could do. She sat still, hoping that it was even remotely helpful. And it seemed to be.

"Thank-you Ellen, that adds confirmation to Hans' theory. It really does seem like the best approach is to keep this quiet. This brings me to..." Claudia turned to Hans. "I trust you have...?"

There was a nod of the head from Hans. "What would you like me to do with them?"

Claudia pondered for a moment and then for a moment more. "I think it would be wise to teach Ellen hand-to-hand combat. If anything, we can find another blacksmith to make up something of her liking and something that is her own."

"Elder Smith is still around. I'm sure he'd take to the task. Heavens knows that I haven't seen him for decades." Hans brushed this off. Everything seemed so casual and Ellen felt so lost.

Claudia clapped her hands together, the obvious look of disappointment on her face. "The fact that he didn't take on a specialisation really irks me. He has so much talent!"

"He does enough for us as it is. And being one of the best blacksmiths available in this day and age already seems like a specialisation to me."

"Wait. Elder Smith was one of us?" Ellen asked, interrupting the backwards and forwards banter.

They both looked at her and spoke at the same time, harbouring the same sentiments. "A good one at that."

Claudia rose from her chair. "I think we discussed what needed to be discussed. Unfortunately, I also have other matters that I need to attend to today. This thing with Dvorak doesn't seem to want to go away and it's causing everyone a headache." She gave Hans a drilling look and Ellen a small wave. She then left the room, leaving the Master and his student in the boardroom.

Hans stood up from his chair, motioning for Ellen to do the same. "Well, let's not waste any time."

- - -

Ellen sat in the training room they used previously and watched as a foot hooked onto the door and dragged it open. A balancing Hans re-entered, carrying several items that were sheaved in black material – silk, perhaps. He delicately placed these down onto a table that had been pushed against the far wall, positioning the item so they were in straight lines next to each other. There were four and they varied greatly in length.

"You will recall earlier," he spoke, sitting down next to Ellen on the edge of a table. "That we spoke about Elder Smith being a man of his craft. Do you also remember that story that I told you about my childhood? About Master Melvin?"

Ellen nodded. Of course she remembered, it seemed fresh in her mind.

"Well. During our sessions together, he used to describe to me about weapons that could be used to kill Necromancers. Hunters used to have them made to very specific, very stringent dimensions to assist them in their endeavours. Now, Hunters don't exist anymore but the weapons do. Whilst it is possible to kill them without these arms, having them makes it very much easier. My first encounter with Master Melvin was in in the blacksmith workshop – one of the best blacksmiths and a man of his craft - and he happened to pick up a long package which he paid very handsomely for."

Ellen watched as Hans reached back and lightly stroked the longest object.

"These weapons were made of silver and had a number of incantations put on them. A dire combination that our darling counterparts really can't stand." He rose to his feet and smiled at Ellen, knowing that he had her hooked on every one of his words. He then picked up the longest of the items and passed it towards Ellen.

"Take this one but take care not to drop it."

She reached her hands out, taking the long item. It had weight to it and she found herself almost dropping it when Hans retracted his hands. But then she readied herself, and held it straight.

"It's heavy, isn't it?"

Hans' eyebrows perked up, his lips twisting into an entertained smile. "What did you expect? You can take it out of its case when you're ready."

Ellen eyed him, unsteadily.

"It doesn't bite you know. Put it down onto the table if you need to."

She moved to the table and placed it on the hard surface. Chink. Then her fingers hovered over the gold cord that held the silk bag closed.

"Come on now..." Hans urged.

She grabbed the cord and unpicked the knot that secured it. She then pushed her fingers into the hole and forced it open. Slowly, she reached inside.

Her fingers brushed against something cold; something hard. It had deep, deep grooves in it – was it a handle? She wrapped her fingers around it and pulled. A long, silver object slithered out from the case. What was it?

"That, my friend, is a katana."

Her eyes lingered on the blade that twinkled in the light and then wandered to the hilt. A cloth was wrapped around the centre however, the rest was clear and exposed a very elaborate pattern. She held it closer to herself, marvelling at workmanship that went into it.

"Careful that you don't poke your eye out with it," laughed Hans, watching on as Ellen analysed every nook; every cranny. He also hadn't seen the weapons out of their cases for a fairly long time. He didn't have any reason to use his Master's weaponry although he did admire the katana. "How about the next one?"

Ellen found it difficult to draw herself away from beauty of the katana but she finally separated herself from it and did the same ritual with the next object. This one was a short sword, stubby compared to the katana and lighter in terms of weight. The detailing was the same as was the high polish finish. The third object was the shortest – a dagger. Whilst it wasn't as majestic as the others, the detailing on the blade itself was equally as fascinating. Swirls were etched into the silver, forming what looked like oriental clouds.

"And then the last item."

Ellen gripped the last item which happened to be heavier than the others, the heaviest by far. She flipped it over and something on it moved, reminding her of a child's abacus. She unfurled the cord and let it drop to the floor. A hauntingly wicked crossbow sat in her arms, being cradled like a newborn.

"Made of only the finest materials. Master Melvin enjoyed his close combat but he also had a soft spot for projectiles and had this made to his very own design. Obviously you can understand why we can't practice using actual weaponry, but we can always learn techniques and moves." He held up to rods of rounded wood, a broom handle that had been sawed in half. He passed one to Ellen, and placed the second half onto the table.

Hans then walked behind Ellen, and ran his hands along her own. Her skin tickled but nevertheless, she let him correct her grips as if it was a hilt. "That's it. And then you do this to strike from the side." He guided her arms through the motion, whispering in her ear.

"And this if you want to parry from an attack." Again, he helped her with the moves.

For the remainder of the afternoon, Hans taught her each and every move he knew, taking turns to attack and to block. It was a kind of dance in the room, their legs and arms moving in synchronisation as they emulated mock fights. Ellen felt the energy dwindle from her body, but she enjoyed this moment together, solidifying their bond further as Master and apprentice.

"She's very skilled indeed." A gruff voice said, almost as if to congratulate Ellen. Hans and Ellen broke their dance and dropped their mock swords, turning to face the doorway. The newcomer had his back to the door, taking in their practice session.

"Elder Smith!" welcomed Hans, as he strode across the room and shook hands with the man.

"I sensed that I would be required. And you must be Ellen." The blacksmith held out his calloused hand to Ellen, to which she reciprocated.

"I heard so much about your skills."

"Years of experience, young one," he smiled. He bowed down, and whispered in her ear: "Watch this." He looked back at Hans, his tongue in his cheek. "Should we get designing then so she can go hunting some of the dark ones?"

Hans stared at the short man in disbelief, his hands flying to his hips and his eyes wide. "That's not the intention, no!"

Laughing, the old man beckoned to the two. "Now, where are those chairs? We have some drawing to do."

Chapter Fifteen

The plush carpet sunk beneath her feet as Ellen left the training room and headed for her living quarters to freshen up, a large smile plastered on her face.

For the past two weeks, they had been working on close combat, the wooden rods leaving angry red lashes on her skin. But this didn't phase her, nor did she mind. They served as a reminder to never be brash, but to be humble. They also showed that every time she had been beat, she would get up and the dance would start over. The lashes and bruises marks of pride; marks of self-determination.

But that all changed today.

She had managed to outmanoeuvre Hans in their final skirmish of the day, forcing him onto his knees after a well-played parry before the wooden pole struck down onto this back. She thought he would have been upset; rather, he looked up at her grinning and clapping his hands.

"Perfect. I need to pitch you up against Claudia next."

And then he gave her a high-five – his hand covered in wraps and hers, in hardened callouses - and let her go for the rest of the afternoon.

Now she found herself wandering the corridors on automatic pilot, humming to herself, in the best mood she had been in for a long while. She replayed the moment in her head, again and again, hoping that everything she learnt would sink inside her and that she would be able to perform if she ever had to. It is one thing to be able to train well, but another if you actually had to use those skills.

She approached the door of her room, opening it and almost doubling back on her steps. Someone – or something – had been in here.

Three packages sat on her bed, wrapped neatly in brown paper and string.

Her mind automatically trailed to the worst case scenario - What if they were malicious? What if it was a trap? Could the same person that injured the mortal man in the park have left these for her?

Her eyes scanned over the wrapping, her attention catching on a white slip of paper that was tucked beneath one of the parcels. There were two sentences - two short sentences - written in fancy yet legible cursive: It's time you had your own. These are yours.

Her head pounded, her breath light and rapid.

Barely being able to contain the excitement, she sat down on the edge of her bed and held the first of the packages in her arm. It was the smallest one and the lightest, and she had a fair idea of what was inside it. Ellen tore off the string and paper, exposing a black cover made of silk and the gold cord. The smile now re-igniting her face, she fumbled with the cord and drew out what was inside, letting it sit in her lap. Her eyes marvelled at the detail; the detail that she only saw on paper during the design phase. It was as if she was a child in a candy store.

The dagger that they had designed whilst cramming their heads together with Elder Smith stared up at her, the blade and hilt both gleaming. Whilst she nearly opted to go for a similar swirl design, she instead chose one that had more Celtic qualities to it, the design running from the tip of the hilt to halfway along the blade. It really was an epitome to brilliant workmanship.

She put this on the bed behind her, taking care not to run any part of her body along the foreboding blade. She then took the second largest parcel, this one being a bit more difficult to lift with one hand, removed the wrappings and the case, and admired the katana that she had opted for. Again, the work that had gone into it was nothing short of breathtaking and she sat admiring it. That was, until she remembered that there was also a third package that awaited her.

The unopened package was the largest and also the widest although it wasn't very heavy. She stood onto her feet, and leaned down over the bed. Her hands shook as she slowly peeled back the paper; in her mind, guessing what it could be.

It couldn't be a crossbow because it was too long and too light.

It couldn't be another sword because again, it was too light.

It didn't take long to establish what the object was. The more she unwrapped it, the more of its componentry became exposed.

The strong yet flexible arc.

The string that ran from one side of the arc to the other.

It was a bow with arrows.

She ran her fingers along the carvings that decorated the wooden arc, each one of them clean and smooth. The wood itself was handsome and dark. She held it closer to her eyes, examining something that was carved on the inside. It was the numbers that made up this year. Ellen spied another note which was tied to the bottom of the bow. As she read it, the year stamp made sense.

As a birth gift. My gift to you.

Putting the bow down with the rest of her newly acquired weaponry, Ellen couldn't help but jump and throw her hands in the air, happiness pumping through her veins like an adrenaline junky about to jump from a great height. She had to thank Hans for the gift and show her appreciation! Realising that Hans would probably still be in his room, she surged across her bedroom and into the hallway. The moment she laid her foot outside of the doorway, she felt a strong pair of hands grip her by the forearms.

"Ellen!" a frightened, woman's voice hissed at her. Ellen looked at the woman who was covered in a dark travellers cloak, her face and eyes hidden by a large hood of the same shade.

"Yes?" Ellen asked, trying to fight against the grip the woman had on her hands. If she didn't let go sometime soon, she was certain the blood flow would be cut. She gave a last attempt, and then let herself go still, giving in.

"I've come to warn you," the woman hissed again, frantically. She loosened her grip, but still clenched onto Ellen's arms so she couldn't escape.

Ellen squinted at her, trying to make sense of what she was saying. She was speaking in riddles; riddles that she didn't understand.

"Would you like to come inside?" Ellen hoped that if they were in a private space, the woman would be comfortable to divulge more information.

The woman glanced around – or so Ellen thought, as her hood moved side to side – and pushed Ellen into her own bedroom before snapping the door shut behind them.

"You must be careful Ellen!" her tone was more relaxed but still on edge. The two women stood in the middle of the bedroom facing each other, a contrast between innocence, and fear and secrecy. One was unmasked and exposed – her identity bare for all to see – and the other, hidden behind coverings and identify skewed.

Was it for the fear of safety?

Ellen stared at her, unsure whether to trust this newcomer. "Who are you?"

The woman shook her head and didn't even make the slightest move towards lowering her hood. "I can't tell you because they will find me. They will kill me. They will kill you."

"Wait. You're not making any sense. Who will kill you and I?" Alarm bells were starting to ring in the back of her head, and her stomach did a flip. She didn't dare to think she was lying, the recent past events dictated otherwise. The threat was real and it was very real. The quicker she could alert Hans and Claudia, the quicker they could be on greater alert and make preparations.

The woman shook her head. It appeared that she wasn't willing to divulge any names. Ellen grew impatient with the woman, crossing her arms and staring at her. Why warn someone if you aren't going to give evidence that you can prepare on? Especially when lives were at risk.

"Is it Dvorak? He is on trial," Ellen told her flatly. Maybe if she kept prodding – mentioning different names – then she can divulge more information.

"No, no Ellen! But you don't know!" she gasped, holding a covered hand up to her face.

"What don't I know?"

"Why, Ellen," her voice quietening back down to a whisper. "Dvorak is innocent!"

Ellen shifted form one foot to the other, becoming uncomfortable. She didn't know what was right or what to believe these days. The truth had become so very twisted that it was difficult to establish what the truth was. "Then who is it?"

The woman moved away from Ellen by a single step. She then let her hands fall to her side, becoming nothing more than just a tall figure with cloth hanging off her frame. Her voice was pleading now. "He has someone working on the inside; someone that is close to you. They are watching your every move." She rushed towards Ellen, grabbed her by the shoulders and then disappeared outside of the room.

By the time Ellen had reached the doorway, the woman had already gone – out of sight.

Sighing from frustration, Ellen made her way through the labyrinth of hallways until she reached the doors of the boardroom and hammered on the wooden panels. There was no reply; she banged again out of desperation.

"Hans, please be there," she pleaded to herself. "Please, I need you."

There was a moment and the heavy door quickly cracked open. Claudia stuck her head out of the gap, and looked down at Ellen through her glasses. "Is this urgent?" she asked, politely but urgently. Her eyes drilled into Ellen.

"Someone visited me. I don't know who it was but they said Dvorak is innocent!"

Claudia pushed on the door, so it was now fully open. Two of the chairs along the table were filled with a third pushed away. Hans and Dvorak sat side by side, whilst Claudia sat opposite them.

"Yes, we know," Hans replied, looking up at her. And then she felt all three pairs of eyes train onto her, Dvorak appearing as the most ragged of the trio. His cheeks were fallen; his eyes had deep, dark patches, and his skin was a sickly yellow shade.

"Wh-what?" Ellen stammered, taking an unconscious step backwards. "But, the trial..."

"The trial concluded this morning after the Seek, analysing the results and several discussions with Master Dvorak himself. He's innocent and has been reinstated to his Master duties."

Dvorak stared from Hans to Claudia, Hans and Claudia again. "This girl can be trusted with such private information?"

Hans held up a palm to quiet Dvorak. "She can be. She's been training with both myself and Claudia and never ceases to amaze us." He gained eye contact with Ellen and she sensed him brimming on the inside but he didn't let his face portray this apart from the slightest upturn at the corners of his lips.

"Ellen," he continued. "I'd like to formally introduce you to Master Dvorak. He knows of our predicament and has most ceremoniously and graciously agreed to give you training in a very specific – a very niche – ability. He will also be working alongside us to protect you and to keep an eye out on things."

Ellen regained her composure, leaning on the back of one of the armchairs.

"And what ability would that be?"

Dvorak cleared his throat, and tapped his fingers on the highly-polished wooden surface. "I specialise in darkness, the underworld. I'm going to attempt to teach you how to detect Necromancers, bury yourself into their minds, control them, torture them and most important," he smiled slyly at Ellen. "How to get them to do your bidding. Essentially, everything that we stand against. The best defence is a strong offense."

And then he started laughing.

Chapter Sixteen

The training room was filled with nothing other than the strictest silence as Ellen stood in one spot, as rigid as she could. She was nervous.

Although she had the freedom to move about, she wasn't sure of Dvorak's training techniques and found it safest to keep still and out of his way. She watched as the beefy, elderly man in front of her scrimmaged through a peeling black suitcase, his back to her. He finally cleared his throat, found what he was looking for and turned to face Ellen. He wasn't much taller than she was but she still found him strangely intimidating.

"They tell me you are good, somewhat of a prodigy and the infamous century-born," he drawled, emphasising every word. He circled his fingers as he spoke as if he was explaining something. In his other hand, he held a long, black piece of cloth which pooled on the ground.

"Well, I don't know about that," she replied. She didn't know what else to see. She didn't want to give the impression that she was arrogant, nor the impression that she was full of self-doubt.

He stared at her, now twirling the cloth with his fingertips. "What I am about to teach you lass, is something not even the best and advanced of our kind can accomplish. Not only is it difficult, but it is also unspoken about as it can be regarded as despicable and a sign of pure evil. If you want to live a full life – if you want to live – I suggest you keep everything we do to yourself. Only you, myself, Hans and Claudia knows what is going on inside this room. If you tell anyone what we are doing, I will deny it and you will be seen the fool and a rotten liar. Am I clear?"

Ellen swallowed hard. She found her hatred for the man growing. He continued with his speech; a speech, she assumed, that was built on his loathing of her.

"They seem to want me to teach you so you can have these tools as part of your arsenal and to protect yourself to greater avail. But we will really see just how talented you are, won't we Miss Winton? Or should we call you Miss Grey as you seem to be his little pet?"

She flinched as he spoke her last name, she flinched again as he spoke about Hans. "Yes sir. I have a question."

He stared at her, his eyes burning with the hate he was inflicting on her. "And what would that be? We haven't even started."

"How are you supposed to teach me how to enter a Necromancer and channel the darkness if there is not a single one in sight?" She pressed onwards. "Or do you happen to be chum-buddies with one in this manor?"

He strode towards her, his face getting redder and redder underneath the dim lighting of the room. She closed her eyes as he lifted a hand to strike her but the strike never came. "I don't give up on hopeless causes like you but another move like that and I will certainly discipline as I see necessary, you stupid little girl."

Ellen opened her eyes to see him lowering his open palm. He then lifted his other hand, the one carrying the piece of material that he had extracted from his briefcase. "This is a blindfold, if you haven't figured out as much. During your training, you will have absolutely no vision because you need to concentrate and focus only on the task at hand. You'll do something wrong either way, but you can't have too much stimulus."

Dvorak walked behind her and put the middle of the cloth across her forehead which spanned down to her nostrils. She was plunged into an uncomfortable darkness,] and her senses went into a state of frenzy. He then pulled tight and knotted the ends together. "You can breathe, yes? Not that it matters to me."

"Yes but," Ellen murmured, running her hands along her forehead wear the blindfold cut into her skin. "It's a bit tight."

"Fantastic. First things first. It's no use teaching you to do anything else, unless you can recognise a Necromancer which means being able to detect them. Tell me, what are the signs that they are near?" She hated not being able to see where he was. Dvorak's voice seemed to drift around the room, floating around her.

And so the lesson spanned over an hour; two hours, and almost three. Ellen's tiredness increased as each minute passed and her ability to concentrate decreased. It was a fight that she was losing, and losing greatly. Reaching the point of frustration, she stopped responding to Dvorak's instruction to regain her composure.

"What do you think you're doing?" he asked. She could tell her was moving towards her as his voice became thundering and almost next to her ear.

"I need rest." It was a cross between a pant from frustration, and a statement from sheer fatigue. Neither Claudia nor Hans trained her this rigorously, for hours at a time. Her focus was wearing thin.

Dvorak laughed, the quietness of it booming louder and louder. "That's because their training methods are weak! My clan is trained only to the highest standards. Tell me you foolish girl. Do you think Lucien rests?"

Ellen didn't say anything. She knew the answer – no – but he didn't want to give him the satisfaction of hearing her say it. It felt that as if he found happiness and glee in making her feel his emotionally-charged hate.

"Well. I asked you a question. Do you?" His patience was wearing thin and his words became more pointed and more deliberate.

"No, sir."

He clapped his hands together close by her, the snap of it making her jump. "Then try again. I want you to bury yourself into me and take over my body. Possess me."

Ellen concentrated as hard as she could, trying to use the last ounces of energy that powered her body. She tried to focus on entering his body – entering his mind – but it did not seem to want to happen. She opted for a change in technique, hoping that it would produce a small linkage at least. Focusing not only on his body, she tried tapping into and channelling the hate that flowed onto her from Dvorak. There was a resurgence and she amplified this energy away from her like a sonic boom.

And almost immediately, she found herself with split vision. Not only was she staring from her own eyes but also from Dvorak's. It was unnerving to see herself standing there in a blindfold and being able to see Dvorak however, it was something she quickly adapted to. She tore off the blindfold so it hung from her neck and raked her thoughts for a command to give him, to truly find out if she had accomplished what he wanted.

Sit down, she ordered on her mind. And so he did, immediately sitting down where he stood. It appeared that he had succumbed to the command without a thought. Stand up. He was now on his feet. Ellen looked at his face, which seemed expressionless.

It appeared that the key to possessing someone was hatred.

She continued projecting her energy and maintaining a strong link, so strong that she now begun to see flashbacks of his past. The first was him as a child, laughing and ripping off the colourful paper from his presents bright and early on Christmas morning. His parents watched onwards, brimming with joy. This scene began to change; another one emerging. Dvorak was now a teenager, a senior, and he was walking through the gates of a school with rubbish and taunts thrown at him. He kept his head bowed and his books clenched close to his chest. It reminded Ellen of herself. The scene changed once more. He was now an adult, him and his family running in the middle of the night through cold, heavy snow. What appeared to be out of nowhere, the unmistakeable man that was Lucien stepped in front of his two children and tore them away. After putting up a hefty fight, like the battle of powers, Dvorak fell to his knees with his hands pushed together and he started sobbing. But it was a pointless exercise. He watched as his two children were taken from him – murdered – in front of his very own eyes.

The Dvorak in front of her – in the room – slowly dropped onto this knees; one first, and then the other. He emitted a pained cry as his hands flew towards his forehead. He rocked back and forth, the strangled cries becoming more and more forced. Ellen's possession of him and her view threw his eyes began to flicker, the connection between them getting weaker. And then it abruptly closed as Dvorak forced her out of his mind. He remained on the floor, his chest heaving now from his expended efforts.

Ellen saw his lips move but struggled to hear the words that he spoke. Once she heard them, she regretted that she could.

"How," he snarled, venom-filled. "How dare you use my memories against me. You are tainted! You are not one of us. You bear all the makings of one of them!"

Sickness, nausea, swept over her and her skin became wet with sweat. The monster named panic started to settle inside her and the room appeared to be getting smaller and tightening around her. Her breathing became shallow and constrained and she couldn't block out Dvorak's cursing no matter how hard she tried. Each word was another stone added in her already heavy heart.

"-are a disgrace to us all. What were they thinking when they-"

She stepped backwards, away from the man in front of her. He was becoming more and more hysterical and she found herself fearing him ever more. She had to get away from him before her instability worsened. Ellen fled from the room, the blindfold still hanging from her neck. She didn't get very far when her body gave way and she found herself sitting in the hallway against the wall. Her face was buried in her hands, and the back of her head rested on the hard-wall behind her. The wooden-panelling of the walls; the navy carpet, the chandeliers seemed to warp around and talk to her. She clenched tight her eyelids, trying to come to her senses.

She wasn't a bad person.

She wasn't a bad person.

Soft, warm fingers gently entangled with hers and she continued to sit with closed eyes. "There comes a time where we all doubt ourselves and our place in the world we live in." A pause. "But the world is ours to make what we want of it. You can spend your time running and letting things hit deeply. Or you can let it go and keep living the way you want. Our life isn't an easy one and you've just begun your journey. You're just a baby and you have a big burden on your shoulders. It will get better."

Ellen angled her head and opened her eyes. Rolland was sitting next to her, his hazel eyes trained on her.

"Why does all this happen to me?" she asked, as if he could answer her question. She knew he couldn't; it was more rhetorical, but she asked anyway. She needed a Guardian now, someone to look out for her when Hans couldn't.

"It should show you that you are something special, something revered. You are one of us, and you were destined for it. If no one believed in you, Hans wouldn't be spending so much time on you. Surely that's an indication and is worth something, right?"

She sighed and started sobbing. The drops ran down her cheek and onto her lips, the saltiness leaving an aftertaste in her quivering mouth. Rolland reached a finger out and wiped a tear that threatened to snake down further. And then he looked away – hastily, guiltily.

"What's wrong?"

He breathed out, refusing to make eye contact with her. His eyes were glued to the carpet in front of him.

"Rolland, what's wrong?" she repeated, urgently.

"You need to be strong," he replied, almost choking on the words. This made Ellen cringe, her instincts kicking into alarm mode. Bells started ringing somewhere in her mind.

Something wasn't right.

He was hiding something.

"What for?" She blinked, flinching. Did she want to hear this at one of her darkest hours? Could she bear to hear it?

"Ellen," he said, clenching onto her hand harder. What went from a warm and gentle grip turned into one of worry and concrete. He finally looked at her, his eyes betraying his composure. "Hans has been taken to trial."

And Ellen's world combusted – collapsed – as she fainted and fell to the ground.

Chapter Seventeen

The atmosphere inside the compound was in a state of confusion and chaos. Did Hans really kill someone and take on a role as a double agent to the Necromancers?

The news of the upcoming trial of the infamous Master Grey had spread like wildfire, like fire taking to dry grass. Since the breaking of the news, peaceful protests had taken place outside of the trial room and Claudia had been inundated with countless letters or disapproval and personal testimonies of Hans as a person. Although Claudia was unable to comment on the situation at hand, Hans had thanked everyone for the support they offered and that he would go to trial without appealing the initial summon. He, just like any other Tempusmancer, was bound by the same law and he expected to go through the same process to determine the truth.

He had nothing to hide.

No one expected lesser nobility from him and the crowd erupted in applause.

There was only one person within the manor that seemed to be bursting with happiness and his words were heard echoing with enthusiasm in the dining room on the morning of the trial. Breakfast was served earlier than usual to cater for those attending the trial and the buffet was freshly stocked with the breakfast selections. Most had filled their plates with little food, unable to eat, and had already returned to their chairs. Ellen was too focused on pushing the eggs and bacon around her plate, trying to comprehend the flurry of events, and blocked out the wining voice. Whilst everyone else sat in solemn silence, a tribute for Hans, Dvorak was pompously voicing his 'humble' opinion that they would finally establish who the real Hans was and see beyond his façade, and this was karma for incriminating him previously. He also added that he hoped the Seek would need to be employed. There was a collective murmur as everyone showed their disapproval; a murmur which stopped when one of the female Tempusmancers had let the best get of her, rose from her seat and slapped Dvorak across the face.

"You dog," she screeched, pointing her finger into his chest. Each jab was stronger than the last, and pushed the man backwards. "You are an abomination. This is a time of need and yet, here you are finding solace in someone else's pain! Have you no shame!"

Someone on the other side of the room had put their hands together, clapping slowly. One by one, the others in the room followed suit, many laughing at the stubby man who now kept his head down so no one could see his cheek which was red and stinging, and also swollen to almost double its size. The sound of a hundred hands clapping was thunderous and music to Ellen's ears. It was the second time Ellen had witnessed him being humiliated and he deserved it. It also gave 'we are one' a new meaning. She was proud of the cohesion – the way everyone came together – in the face of difficulty and to protect one of their own. She was also thankful that she was no longer regarded as an outcast and had been invited to join members of Hans' clan for meals. She was no longer alone.

"You've hardly touched your meal," the woman next to told Ellen kindly. The woman was regarded as somewhat of the grandmother of the clan. Although it was an unspoken rule to never ask ages, the general consensus agreed that she was at least two hundred years old. This was established off the comparison to others and their recollections of who they had observed in the manor during their time.

"I'm not hungry. I can't eat," she replied dully, stabbing the bacon with her fork before laying it down on the side of her plate.

"Nonsense, nothing to worry about," one of the others spoke. He had a thick accent to his words and twirling his fork so much that he nearly impaled his neighbour onto it.

"Oi! Watch where you're pointing that thing, would you? Lethal, even with a fork! My word, they really have dropped their standards to let you in, didn't they? You'd think they'd make you master forks before they give you the incantation." The table erupted in laughter as the neighbour poked his tongue to the side in his cheek and held up his arms as if to surrender.

"What was I saying? Oh, yes. Hans has been through a few trials before and he came out fine. That, and he's made of some sturdy stuff. His Master was truly something and for Hans to learn under him would have been amazing and he's seen some pretty nasty stuff as his time as Grand Master. You can't forget that. He's like a saint walking between peasants."

The man's neighbour dropped his jaw, gaping at the accented man. "Did you just call me a peasant, peasant? That's offensive! I'll have you know I was part royalty!"

Laughter, yet again.

"Yes, royalty of the Kingdom of the Great Toilet. That really is something to be proud about. I consider peasant to be a welcome step up for you."

Ellen couldn't help it, a grin threatening to break onto her lips. And then it did, and the smile spanning from ear to ear. It was a clever diversion; a diversion that was working.

"Boys, please," the grandmother quipped but there was no denying the amusement in her voice either. "That's not table talk."

- - -

"I'm sorry you can't come with us dear, but orders are orders." The elderly woman pulled Ellen into a hug before releasing her. A personal request from Hans was to bar Ellen from attending the trial and this time it was upheld and supported unanimously. It was agreed that she didn't need the added stress in her life. They were now standing in the doorway of the dining room, Ellen about to go one way and the clan going the other.

"Yes, dear Ellen. You can spend your time wondering about how to be ruler of a Great Toilet empire!" The two men punched each other on the arms before taking Ellen into a headlock and ruffling her hair. It was clear who the jokers were amongst them.

"Don't worry. It will be over quickly. There are things you can do to take your minds off it and we will visit you as soon as we can. I believe Guardian Rolland won't be attending the trial either. You may be able to give him company and gain experience."

Ellen nodded her head, although it was just a nod to keep them happy. The less she had to do with Rolland, the better she deemed it to be. She still hadn't fully recovered from his accusation that she had killed someone.

"That man is just weird. Don't ever be married to your specialisation," the man with the accent cautioned, "because you will end up just like him. If you ever fall in love with your job, just take a good, hard look at him."

More laughter, and the swing of an arm as the grandmother clapped him around the head. The laughter died off, the man rubbing the side of his head.

"Take care," she said to Ellen sternly. And then they left down the corridor, leaving Ellen alone. Oh how she wished was able to be there. But she respected Hans' wish and dispersed the idea of sneaking into the trial room.

She wandered down the corridors at a leisurely pace, letting the carpet steer her with no real direction. Opting to immerse herself in a book, Ellen changed her heading for the library. The library had to be one of her favourite places in the manor; the high ceilings that were supported by rich, mahogany wood, the carpet that was softer and fuller than that throughout the others rooms; the lines upon lines of book that was almost roof high. She found it the most comforting place at the time of need with its smell of aged books and large, leather armchairs placed in private areas for privacy. Ellen strolled through the door, and let the atmosphere of the room take over her senses.

Already knowing the relative location of every genre, she ambled to the left where the fictional novels were separate from non-fiction. She was hoping that she would have the library to herself with everyone attending the trial but this was not true and she was not alone. The man that she wanted to see the least of all in the manor was standing on one of the bookcase ladders, running his fingers along the spines of the books. She wanted to trace her steps backwards and disappear but he had already noticed her.

"Isn't it a shame," Rolland stammered, absentmindedly, "that the books can't tell us everything that we need to know, everything that we need to look out for in life. It would make things so much simpler in life."

Ellen folded her arms and bit her lips. She wasn't quite sure where he was not going with this nor was she very interested in what he had to say. He had a way of speaking in riddles and if he wasn't speaking in riddles, he was the bringer of bad news.

"Why aren't you at the trial?"

Rolland looked at her. "I've been around Hans long enough to know that he will come out of it just fine." He eyeballed her for a minute and then went back to scanning through the books.

"But you worked with him closely. Why aren't you there to at least support him?"

His hand paused but his eyes remained trained on the titles. "Ellen, I don't need to be everywhere where he is. And I've seen my fair share of him over the years. He's not half as innocent as you think, you know. Oh, definitely not."

"If he isn't so innocent, then why are so many of our kind protesting against the trial and supporting him?"

He finally found the book he was searching for and pulled it out of its place. He looked over at her, a lulling look on his face and a small yet sinister smile. "Everyone needs something to believe in. And in case you haven't noticed, he's a bit of a rockstar amongst us."

He leaped off the ladder; the carpet muffling what should have been a loud thump. He then took small steps – baby – steps towards Ellen, the book held tightly to his chest so she couldn't read the title.

"I have an interesting case I need to attend to, one that you might be interested in. Whilst the trial is happening, at least it would give you something to do."

"What is it about?" she asked curiously. She was hesitant with the proposition, but if it meant it would ease the throbbing entity that was her mind, she would take it. Even if it did mean that she would be stuck with Rolland for a while longer.

"One of our kind has been caught meddling with darkness in public. Something like this only comes up every decade or so. You wouldn't want to miss this. You'd be stupid to miss this."

Ellen mulled it over, weighing up the pros and cons. She couldn't stand the man and his arrogant demeanour but everyone kept advising her to get as much experience and exposure as she could. And if Hans trusted him, doesn't that mean that she can too? Almost as if reading her mind, Rolland was the first to break the silence.

"I'll see you in the entrance hall in twenty minutes."

Chapter Eighteen

By time Ellen had descended the grand staircase which led to the entrance hall, Rolland was already there, staring at his feet and waiting for her. He shuffled at something on the carpet but look up as Ellen bounced off the last of the steps.

"Right on time. But before we go, I feel like we need to talk about what you may see today."

He motioned towards a cluster of chairs that was placed near a large window that opened to views of the grounds. It streamed through the morning sunlight, making all metallic surfaces glow and shine majestically. The hall was cavernous like all other areas of the manor but the wall-like windows made it lighter and welcoming. It was an open room and usually acted as a hub teeming with visiting Tempusmancers that were coming and going. There were several groups of chairs placed around coffee tables, larger tables for those that had large documents they wanted to show their peers and a drinks bar to accommodate those that were needed something extra whilst they waited or worked. It was a hive this morning as everyone arrived, the foot-traffic and arrivals since dying down. Now it was just Rolland

and Ellen and another duo of what appeared to be business men enjoying a freshly brewed coffee and talking quietly between themselves.

Ellen sat down in the closest seat to the window, enjoying the warmth as the light shone on her legs. Rolland took the chair opposite to her and leaned in, as if there were others that were listening in. This made sense, the words of Dvorak flooding back to her.

... it is also unspoken about as it can be regarded as despicable and a sign of pure evil...

"What we are about to do is highly dangerous and the situation can change within a split second. Those that delve within Necromancer business are usually unpredictable at best and aren't afraid to kill if they feel threatened. In some cases, they kill just because they can."

Ellen looked onwards patiently, folding her hands on her crossed legs. What he was saying wasn't anything new. He pressed further.

"When we arrive back, you cannot speak about this to anyone – anyone. The darkness is not something to be spoken about, even if you are on our side and merely doing a job. The darkness, Necromancers, represents a very bad place for many of us here, and a good portion has lost loved ones to them."

He swallowed hard, as if he found it difficult to go on.

"For a lot of Tempusmancers, if you are willing to talk about the darkness, they will assume that you are at arms with them; they believe that you will go after their families. You automatically become the symbol and omen for death."

Ellen sat back, the urgency of secrecy become increasingly clear. "I can do that."

Rolland smiled, reassured. "Great."

He pulled out a folded piece of paper from his pocket, and smoothed it out on the coffee table between them. The paper was well crumpled, the creases not wanting to life flat on the glass surface. Ellen could make out that it was a map; a convoluted labyrinth of streets and alleyways. He pointed at a site just to the north of the city centre.

"I don't know if you've ever been to Dawns Hollow but this is our area of interest for today. The city itself is well known to both classes as it has seen its fair share of wars. The outer suburbs are the only sites that did not require any rebuilding after conflicts. A lot of history and a lot of high emotions. As you can imagine, there are a high number of Tempusmancers that reside here. I wonder if you can tell me what other feature this city may have? Take as long as you need, although do bear in mind we will need to leave eventually."

Ellen pulled the map closer to her and took in the delicate detailing. It was an old map, one that was hand-drawn before the rise of technology. She looked for patterns, signs, anything that would catch her attention. But she couldn't find anything out of the ordinary.

"Give up?" asked Rolland, curiously.

"Yes," she sighed. She hated not knowing something or being able to figure things out for herself.

"Dawns Hollow has a high abundance of..." A deliberate pause; a tension builder. "Cemeteries. Can you tell me why Necromancers love cemeteries and why a lot of their activities are more frequent in these areas?"

Ellen scratched her head, knowing that the answer would be obvious.

"Think about what traditionally Necromancers are known for. What have you read about them in books?"

"Necromancers are known for...Oh." Her face fell as the truth hit home. The magnitude of the task she was invited to grew to a much greater size and the importance and risks seemed even more real and complex. She took a deep breath to calm herself down.

"Necromancers mainly have the ability to control the dead, that is their sole purpose. They have evolved their skills slightly throughout the centuries but they are still elementary, nowhere near as complex and able as us. Whilst we should be okay to deal with one or two but if Lucien shows up, that's when we will be in trouble and may need to call for extras or if it's bad, for Guards. Guards are better able to deal with such situations. When we are on the ground, the danger will never go away. Those bodies that are buried can be resurrected awfully quickly."

There was a brief moment as they comprehended the situation within themselves: Ellen, the storm that she is about to fly into and the seriousness of the journey ahead; Rolland, the task of protecting her and keeping her from harm's way. Her head throbbed from the tension. But she was strong. And although her Master was on trial for murder and being an alleged double agent, she couldn't let it affect her.

It was time to be brave.

It was time to live up to her name.

"Would you like something to drink before we head off?"

Ellen felt nausea in her stomach, as if she was on a wildly rocking boat. Her head was spinning and her breathing became shallower.

"Would that be okay? Just a quick tea to settle myself." Rolland nodded and scurried off towards the waiting beverage-hand. She rubbed her temples to calm herself down.

Calm blue oceans.

Calm blue oceans.

And then there was a chink as the Guardian placed the teacup in front of her and reclaimed his seat.

"Rolland. When you said that Hans wasn't as innocent as I thought, what did you mean?" She gazed at Rolland who fell silent for a minute, trying to find his words. He then spoke quickly, quietly.

"Throughout my time here, I have seen him make mistakes, and decisions which were rash and ill-thought out. Don't take me wrong, the man is a genius and is amazing in his own right but that's not to say that he is perfect. He's guided us through a number of wars, of which I am of the impression that he could have minimised casualties. But no. He decided on the method of defence and because of it, more people died than was necessary."

She drank deeply from the cup, letting what was said to be processed. Ellen could have sworn that she heard jealousy in his words; in his tone of voice. Instead of highlighting his finer achievements, Rolland was quick to jump on all the negative aspects. 'Let bygones be bygones', her father would always tell her.

Did he once vie for the Master role or Grand Master?

Was he constantly overlooked for more important roles?

Or was it that he was still angry about the warning he had received?

But nothing prepared her for the question that was coming; which came when Rolland opened his lips. "Are you ready?"

Chapter Nineteen

Rolland was first to appear, with Ellen close on his tail. He had chosen a derelict alleyway as their destination.

The once proud gothic-like buildings with their spires, gargoyles and glass panels were reduced to rubble, obvious scars from previous wars which they neglected to rebuild or had left as a testament to history. It was saddening that such marvels were deduced to nothing, even more saddening that the wars that seemed to occur so often were almost undertaken for superiority cleansing. There was no harmony, and the scene in front of Ellen demonstrated that. She took a rugged step forward, taking the ruins in. The blue sky overhead was bright and chirpy – a dire, teasing contrast of depression and happiness.

"This is so sad," she whispered, her eyes running along bent pieces of metal and broken concrete. "I have no faith."

"Now you see what war and rampage can do to a city. Now you can see why you must never talk about darkness. I can assure you that the damage is not just aesthetic, but runs through the citizens too." He ran his fingers along some of the ruins. "I have fond memories of this place, my grandparents had a house here. It was a gorgeous city and very alluring to the eyes. But now, we must press on."

He wrapped an arm around Ellen's shoulders and guided her out of the damaged alleyway. They turned another corner and were met by a sudden change of scenery. The rubble remained behind them; in front of them, tall modern buildings which were a mix of paned glass and elegant metal. The change was so succinct that it was as if they had just passed into another world. There was no sign of conflict past.

Ellen struggled to combat the oncoming foot traffic. There were throngs of people, a herd which seemed to draw her in amongst them and take her with them. It was so thick that the faces of the people seemed to blend in with each other – a faceless crowd. Rolland grabbed her arm and pulled her behind him.

"Try and stay close," he whispered to her, walking and dividing the crowd around them.

"Why are there so many people?" she asked alarmed and wide-eyed. The last she had been in a crowd so massive was when her stalker – one of Lucien's henchmen – had appeared to be in a car accident. And that was something she would rather put behind her, to suppress that painful memory. "Did something happen?"

Rolland proceeded pushing through the pedestrians, most of them not even realising he was there. He must have been bending reality with every step they made. He finally replied, through clenched teeth. "This is peak hour in the morning. It's normal."

She felt slightly like a fool but it was short lived. They erupted into a thinner crowd, who were more relaxed and strolling rather than power-walking.

"We're nearly there," he added. "This is more of a shopping destination for tourists." They lessened their pace to be more natural, and Ellen was finally able to catch her breath. Whilst there were still plenty of people around them, they didn't appear to be in a rush to get somewhere. Most had food or coffee in hand, some waiting patiently outside of an interesting boutique or shop to open.

And then a moment of sudden realisation. "Rolland, I realised. You didn't actually tell me what we are attending to?"

"Someone tried to practise other abilities and summon someone who shouldn't be summoned. You know what I'm saying?"

"Oh." An instant wave of regret washed over her. She really shouldn't have come. She looked up at the pristine sky which seemed to mock her. "Are you sure I should be here?"

He looked back at her and then looked away. "I don't expect much to happen. You will be fine. Ah, here we go."

Rolland guided her into a smaller street which was well landscaped and maintained. Smaller, newer trees were planted along the side of the road offering nature and greenery amongst the man-made environment. Tall buildings surrounded them, a mix of both new and old, historical creations. All of this caught Ellen's eye but not as much as the one that was at the end of the street. It was the grandest of them all, and dwarfed both of them in its height and glory. It reminded her of a castle, with turrets, smaller windows, and made of stone. Like those that were brought to ruin, this one had elements of gothic influence.

"That," Rolland pointed. "Used to be a satellite meeting point for us. But now, after the fights, it is a museum about medieval times and sorcery. What better place to summon the lord of darkness than something that holds significance to us, right? Very fitting."

He closed his eyes, the colour draining from his face; turning a ghastly pale.

Ellen watched and grew with worry. "Are you okay?" He looked sick; unhealthy.

"I'm fine." He smiled and the colour returned immediately.

"So," Ellen said nervously, her voice quivering. "What are we waiting for?"

"I'm trying to pick up on anything, if there is something out of the ordinary. And," he added, laughing. "There it is." His laugh and smile disappeared, replaced by nothing but coldness and seriousness. He locked eyes with Ellen, his eyes deathlike and all warmness had vanished.

And then she shuddered, her skin prickling up in small lumps.

The sign was unmistakable.

Ellen almost swore that her body was plunged into an ice bath and her energy drained away from her. Trembling, she saw the lights in the shop at the end of the narrow street go out plunging the shop-keep into sudden curiosity and a bout of head scratching. She wanted to break into a run but her feet wouldn't let her. They were anchored to the concrete; the trapped feeling making panic resurface within her. Her head became light, threatening to make her faint unless she managed to regain control of her breathing and body. She tried to scream but her throat was clamped. Even if she could, she doubted anyone would come to her aid. The street would be sealed to pedestrians and no one would hear her.

She tried to refocus on the training that Dvorak had taught her, to possess someone. She closed her eyes, concentrating all her might on Rolland. Ellen let the hate she felt channel through her body. There was a small vibration which indicated that she was close to achieving her goal but everything it came, it fell away. Rolland was fighting back; fighting against her.

Ellen looked behind Rolland where a concentration of black mist had ascended. And then this disappeared, to reveal a man. He took slow steps towards Ellen, the distance closing with each one he made. Ellen hated everything about him, from his pale skin to his short, black hair. His robes swung behind him, the ivy green and gold shimmering with every move. His face had broken into a massive grin, and he clapped his hands together to the non-existent audience.

"Bravo!" Lucien drawled. "Bravo! I dare say, you've managed to keep away for so long. But now here we are. You just couldn't stay away from me, could you?"

He placed a gloved hand on Rolland's shoulder and then sidestepped him. He kept moving towards her, slithering towards her like a snake.

He was five metres from her.

Four metres.

Three.

Two.

One metre.

And then he was so close that his nose brushed up against hers. There was a tingle as his breath hit the skin on her face and he lifted one his hands; his fingers delicately brushing along her cheekbones.

"There is no need to blush," he mused. "You are mine after all."

Chapter Twenty

His touch against her skin left her veins feeling as if they were carrying icy water, complete with shards of ice. She looked away, trying to get away from his fingers but they followed. They were inescapable, they were like magnets.

"Hans Grey can't protect everyone," he laughed. "Oh, look at you. Helpless and so exquisite." His eyes were gentle, and longing.

"You're a monster," she spat, the projectile landing near his shoes. "You are a monster!"

Rolland and Lucien look at each other, trading amusement between them. And then Lucien changed his gaze back to Ellen. His eyes were menacing and haunting however, his voice was sweet and sing-song; what you would expect of two long-time lovers.

"Tell me, dear Ellen. Why am I a monster?" He folded his arms and displaced his weight to one leg. He waited, his robe blowing in a small breeze. She cursed within herself that such a lovely day seemed to be mocking the dire event unfolding in front of them.

She tried to fight the hold Rolland had over her again but still no luck. He didn't even flinch or acknowledge that she was trying.

"My dearest, fighting against Ranger is pointless and your effort is best saved. He's one of the best Necromancers we have. He's our equivalent to your Hans. Now, where were we? Ah, yes, that's right. Why am I a monster?"

She swallowed, not wanting to answer someone as despicable as him. But she did so anyway. "You kill innocent people, you rip apart families, and you thrive on death. Need I go on?"

They both laughed again, the laughter infuriating Ellen. He was a cold hearted murderer. How could he find humour in such a thing?

"You are so naïve. We are trying to advance our kind and everyone who we deal with seems bent on stopping our progress. Is it that wrong to want to progress from something that we remained at for as long as records have been kept? Is it?" He reached his arms out, like he was welcoming guests to a house party, a house party that had figures of death as guests and torture as a main meal.

"Look at the mortals – look at them. We are no different to them! They rape; they pillage, they kill their own kind in the name of progress. They even damage their environment on which they rely on; they damage the hand that feeds. Now, tell me that we are worse."

Ellen knew that he had her cornered with a solid argument. Everything that he had said rung true.

"See," he told her, the one word cutting and carving wounds inside her. "We aren't so different."

There was movement behind Lucien as Ranger – the man masked as Rolland – starting shifting on his feet nervously. "My Lord, can I have a private word?"

Lucien cast a glance over to him. "Yes?"

"I really think this should be kept amongst us two without the privy ears of Miss over there." He jabbed his finger in Ellen's direction. Sighing, Lucien walked over to the waiting Ranger who appeared to be getting more and more alert as time drifted by. He bent down so his ear was level with Ranger's lips.

Still within the hold of the man, Ellen couldn't listen in to the conversation. All she could hear was quit whispering, not enough to establish words. The whispering concluded a minute later, Lucien standing back to his full height.

"Ranger, keep tracking. We can make preparations when the time is right. For now, there are people I would like Ellen to meet."

He turned back to face her; his facial emotions, all too sweet. He cleared his throat. "Ellen, I know how much you miss your parents so thought I may be as kind to let you have a moment with them. It may be your last."

The two figures of her mother and father materialised beside Lucien. He then stepped away, backwards so they were in front of him. Ellen was aware that this was a mind game – nothing more than an example of the powers that Necromancers manifested and to make her vulnerable – but she was too weak and let the threatening emotions take a hold. She let the tears roll down her cheek.

They appeared exactly how she had burned them into her mind. Ellen had her father's eyes, and her mother's hair and smile. Her father had his hand around her mother's waist, both of them beaming down at her.

"We are proud of you," her father spoke, filled with pride. Her mother nodded in agreeance, never being the lady of many words. Ellen could feel herself caving in to the emotions, lead sinking in her heart. She blinked to keep herself from breaking down into a crying wreck.

"Did it hurt?" she asked. She wanted to feel comforted; she wanted to know that they didn't suffer.

They shook their heads. "No. It was quick and we didn't feel a thing, not even a bristle."

Their outlines began to shimmer. With each shimmer, they became increasingly transparent. She could see through them and see Lucien and Ranger waiting.

They opened their mouths for their final words: "Do what you need to do. Do what is right."

And then they disappeared, leaving the trio standing in the empty street.

Lucien clapped his hands again. "Do what is right," he quoted.

Venom filled Ellen, her blood pumping fire and boiling lava as she listened to the man recite her parents' words. How dare he use them against her!

But then, she considered the depth of the words, deducing the sentence to what her parents really wanted. It wouldn't have been to support Lucien in his power-hungry quest. It wouldn't have been to give in because that wasn't right by any standards. She found strength and excitement as she came to terms with the meaning. They wanted her to fight for the Tempusmancers; to make a stand. They saw in her what Hans did, what Claudia did, and what her fellow clan members did.

She smirked to herself and let the new found power and the already existing hate flow through her body. There was no denying that the hate was strong – fiercely strong – but the courage and tenacity that bloomed inside her was enough to overpower it. She wasn't going to give in to the dark side if she could help it; that wasn't like her.

Ellen mustered the hate, controlling it on Ranger. She imagined creeping into his mind, taking over his body and controlling him. The connection weakened and she felt the vibration become more and more prominent. All of a sudden, she saw her split vision come up, one of them staring at Ranger and the other staring at her. She started combing through his mind, combing through for painful memories. One stood out most particular and she lingered on this one hoping that it was one that would work to her advantage.

She watched, replaying the moment that his father died at Lucien's hand and her mother gets taken away for the entertainment of other Necromancers. When he had recounted this story to her all those days ago, it seemed to have moved him. Keeping this link going, she hoped and imagined that Ranger would break down; that he would become weak. If she could keep the parallel abilities strong, maybe she had a chance.

Ellen watched the Ranger in front of her cringe and writher in discomfort.

"Stop!" he shrieked in obvious pain. "Stop."

He stared at her and felt him shunting her out of his mind. Lucien, realising what was happening, stormed up and grabbed her by the hair, kicking her knees to force her to kneel. The linkage was immediately lost. Her knees hit against the rocky bitumen, the sharp little surfaces cutting into her skin.

"That was a bad idea," he whispered in her ear, amused but threatening at the same time.

He shot a quick glance at Ranger. "Are you okay? Do you want me to help you up? Do you want time to have a cry?" he asked mockingly. His tone then changed; he was fierce and impatient. "She's just a little girl. Compose yourself!"

Lucien shifted his grip from tugging at Ellen's hair to her upper arm.

"What's the latest?" he demanded.

A recomposed Ranger held his fingers to his forehead, closing his eyes. A minute had passed before he reopened them. He was calm but there was a sense of urgency in his voice. "They're close by. Incoming in approximately two minutes."

His lord emitted a bitter laugh, Ellen able to feel his body shake. After all the lies and treachery since her rebirth, she wasn't sure of what to expect. She deeply hoped that it a clan of Tempusmancers but she wasn't positive; especially with the betrayal of Ranger and his bluffs all along.

"You know what to do," instructed Lucien.

Ranger closed his eyes once more, his mouth moving quickly and quietly. He was incanting an unknown incantation. The light breeze ruffled his hair and his clothes.

"I'm so sorry," Lucien whispered to her again. There was movement and his hand trembled that held onto her; her being blind as he was standing behind her. Suddenly, she something cold and hard was pressed against her throat – something sharp.

She didn't need to see it to know that it was a blade of some sort.

Ellen closed her eyes, her memory going back to the day which Hans told her to wish for him through thoughts. She hoped that the communication lines were still open; she hoped that Ranger didn't have the ability to tap into it and stop communication.

Hans, if you can hear me and you are coming, please be careful. I just hope I come out of this. They have Rolland monitoring your whereabouts I think.

There was the usual silence; the usual silence which she dreaded each and every time. The darkness that filled her vision was oddly calming and brought her to greater ease. That was, until she heard something which almost made her jump. She had to beat the sudden surprise.

I can see everything. Take care, and I will see you soon.

Hans' voice, his sweet, calming and musical voice! She smirked to herself, feeling slightly more hopeful.

And hoping that it was nothing but pure coincidence and Lucien couldn't hear her, she swallowed as her captor whispered: "And now we wait."

Chapter Twenty-One

The side-street was filled with electrified tension to complement the deafening silent, the only sound being the ruffling of fresh leaves as the breeze passed through the trees. It was a cool day, and the sun was being threatened by slow gathering clouds. It was an accurate mood setting for what was unfolding underneath the blanket of the heavens although it seemed to assist in painting a scene from a hostage-taking novel.

Ellen cursed. The bitumen that she was forced to kneel on proved to be painful as the small rocks cut into the skin on her knees. If her skin wasn't broken and blood hadn't been shed yet, she assumed that it was only a short period away. But this was only small compared to the broader reality.

The blade that was pushed against the tender skin of her neck grew more and more threatening as time continued to trickle by, each second becoming more pronounced than that which preceded it. Lucien's hand which gripped the knife remain poised and still, ready to draw a line in her skin with just a quick pull of his arm. The lingering of the metal on her skin was enough to remind her that it was there; that it was a significant threat and one simple slip could spell life or death.

Ellen kneeled with her head angled down towards the ground, her eyes remaining open and darting in each direction trying to detect further movement around her.

Soon, she hoped. Soon.

Ranger hadn't moved from his position, resting in the ease position. His legs were spread shoulder-width apart forming a triangle and his arms were folded behind his back. The only moving part of his body was his lips which hadn't ceased since Lucien originally gave his command. Lucien himself remained behind Ellen, his robe occasionally pushing against the small of her back.

And then she saw Ranger suddenly shift his stance, now looking more alert than before.

"My Lord, they have arrived," he called shrilly.

"How many of them are there?" Lucien asked, curiously. The blade shifted precariously, Ellen hoping that it would stop moving as the pressure increased on her neck.

There was a brief moment of quietness as Ranger counted. "A few. Wait. Seven."

"Who are they?"

Further silence.

"Claudia, Hans, and three other members that I identify from his clan. It seems that Dvorak has also been kind enough to join the party."

"Dvorak? Why would Dvorak be there? Is he coming back to complete unfinished business?" There was an air of surprised in Lucien's questions. He didn't seem to expect Dvorak to join them on this endeavour.

"I can't seem to get a glimpse into him, I don't know for sure," Ranger sighed frustrated. He then kicked the ground in front of him; a few of the small rocks acting like projectiles and hitting Ellen in the face. "He's collapsed the linkage that I've had. I'm blind, I've lost everything! They're running silent!"

There was movement as Lucien swayed side-to-side; from foot-to-foot.

"Well, regain it!" he snapped.

"But, but...I can't. He's appearing to be a shield for all of them!"

"Ranger. Re-establish the connection or run from me because I will come looking for you. Once I find you, I will tear you apart limb for limb and make sure you're alive to see it happen. I might even head in a bit of hellfire to make things more interesting for me. A much worse fate than your parents, I believe. Understood?" Lucien's words acted as a guillotine over Ranger's head and there was no doubt that he would carry out his threat.

The quivering man shook his head and channelled all the energy he could muster to the task. His forehead was furrowed; his eyebrows clenched together in desperation. As he tackled the task, other figures seemed to materialise around them, humans that looked sickly pale and soulless.

They appeared to be the dead whom Necromancers were well known to be able to summon and possess.

Many of them were dressed in various styles of clothing which reflected a wide number of decades, ranging from the royal garments of the sixteenth century to that of today. There were also many ages, from the elderly to young, precious children. It seemed to be a reflection of their life-state when they had crossed the bridge and were greeted at deaths door with a clap on the shoulder.

Ellen tried to count them all, her final estimates putting them around the 40 mark. She mentally balanced the odds – seven against 40. The odds weren't in their favour; at least, without knowing what her saviours had planned. They possibly would have known this was coming or were already controlling and fabricating the future ahead of them. They had to defeat Lucien's own little army.

"At least you did something right Ranger," Lucien growled. She heard him clear his throat, the blade becoming slightly less pressured against her skin.

"My dearly beloved comrades!" he began as if he was addressing an esteemed audience. "Today – right now – I need you to help me to accomplish a great feat; a feat which could progress our kind! There are scum amongst us that want to see us dead and our race eliminated. Now is your chance to stand as one with us to become our equals! I implore you to attack with full force and tenacity that you can muster. They should not come out of this alive. Let your thoughts wander to your heart's content on how to dispose of this vermin. Play with them if you like. It's open-season!"

He clapped his hands and the figures lurched on their feet, dispersing in each and every direction. A large group of them instantly moved towards the historic building at the end of the street, drifting quietly along the road. Ellen shivered as she realised that they were all transparent to that akin of a ghost in books. One walked through her, and she felt every inch of life drain from her. But this was quickly restored once the deathly figure had passed.

She watched on as the figures vanished one by one. And then there was a puff of black mist that soared into the air, the particles getting carried away by the wind.

And another.

And another.

Followed by another.

"My Lord, they are fighting back!" Ranger shouted hesitantly. The war had started and his minions were being annihilated by scores.

"You think I don't see that?" spat Lucien, his grip tightening around the handle of the blade. The blood had stopped circulating; his knuckles beginning to go white. Was he frightened that they were being defeated?

Ellen let out a laugh which infuriated Lucien even more.

"What are you laughing at, girl?" he demanded.

She let out another chuckle and licked her lips. "I'm laughing because it appears that you're losing. I hope you're not a sore loser or this could be embarrassing for you."

He ran a finger along her jawline and then her hairline. She then felt him lean over her, and plant his lips softly on her cheek.

"But dear. You seem to forget that I have you. I hold the power right now. One single move out of line, and you'll become just another body for me to control and another one of their has-beens." He gave her yet another kiss and then straightened back up. "As far as I am concerned, I am the one winning right now."

And then there was a rumble of low thunder in the distance and drops of rain began to fall. The sky was crying with her and each of the teardrops that fell from heaven covered one of Ellen's own.

Chapter Twenty-Two

The cold raindrops soaked into Ellen's clothes, the sodden material clinging in patches all over her body. She closed her eyes and let it run down her face, finding it an oddly soothing sensation and offering her serenity amidst the chaos surrounding her.

Her eyes lay ahead on Ranger who was still standing in front her, shifting from foot to foot as if standing on one was painful. He appeared to be nervous; nervous and desperate. Nervous because a battle was just beginning – one which could go down in history books – and desperate because he wanted to live.

No one took Lucien's threats lightly because they knew he was a man of his word. If he said he will take someone's life, he will do it. There was no doubt about it.

Ranger's face was contorted together, the nerves which ran through his face twitching sporadically. He was evidently trying with everything he had to re-establish some sort of connection between himself and one of the new arrivals. If he could generate even the smallest link, he would at least have insight into their enemy's locations and immediate plans. This information may be all they need –

the key – to winning this battle, and to progress their power-hungry agenda.

He moved suddenly, his palms flying to his forehead almost comically.

"My Lord!" he called, sounding breathless; the same breathless you would expect from someone who had just finished running a marathon. "One of them has come out of the shield! He's coming towards us now!"

Ellen sucked in her breath, her stomach taking a tumble. Why were they doing this? They were putting themselves in the firing line to get killed!

Her mind raced to Hans and his nobility and selflessness, his tendency to be there for her at all times. She had already dragged him in the labyrinth of Lucien's compound once. She didn't want to be the damsel in distress once again. That wasn't who she was!

The spotlight then moved onto Claudia, the Grand Master that went to all odds to protect her and to mentor her in addition to Hans. Her boldness, her tenacity to fight what was right. The others back at the manor needed her.

And yet here they were, risking everything to come to save her. It made her feel guilty; guiltiness which she didn't want to feel. But then came another thought: she couldn't think of reason why Dvorak would have come for the ride given their last meeting. Unless they required his specialised skills which would be the most logical explanation.

"And who is it?" Lucien asked, the hint of triumph in his voice. Ellen snapped out of her trance, grounding her and bringing her back to reality. The moment was unfolding and it was unfolding quickly. She was powerless and couldn't do anything about it.

Ranger opened his mouth again, his lips parting to say a name which she thought she would never hear.

"It's Dvorak."

Ellen blinked, trying to make sense of it all. Did Dvorak want to complete unfinished business and avenge his children's deaths? Or was it all part of a greater plan?

Lucien himself seemed surprised, almost doing a double take and balking when he had heard the name. She heard him quickly dispel air through his nose; a faint emotion of disbelief.

"And why would he want to do that?"

"Why don't you ask him yourself? He's walking up behind you." Ranger reached up with one of his arms and pointed to something behind his superior.

Lucien edged around Ellen, the knife blade still held firmly against her neck. Her face was now between the crooks in his knees, his body acting as a form of shelter from the falling rain. She suddenly realised that she was cold and shivers surged throughout her entire body. They became uncontrollable, like convulsions.

"Dvorak, my dear boy!" he yelled out, his voice echoing in the street and bouncing off the buildings. Immediately, the street seemed to be smaller and more constrained than it actually was. His hands fumbled and added more pressure to the blade. She swallowed as she contended with the thought of her blood being drawn. She heard faint, slow footsteps which grew louder as they approached.

"I'm not your dear boy". There was no mistaking the long drawl and lack of emotion. Dvorak really was here. "I was never your dear boy."

Lucien mocked the man's pain, acting shocked and hurt.

"Well, can't we let bygones be bygones between us? It was only something small. Let's not that ruin things."

"You call killing my children something small?" Dvorak asked. Ellen gave him credit for keeping so calm; so composed. She certainly could have learned from his book if she didn't despise the man as much as she did.

"Now, now. That was a mistake."

"Mistake?" He was still calm but the directness of his words had increased. "A mistake?"

Lucien's grip tightened around the grip once more. "I'm glad we reached an understanding."

There was a growing tension between the two highly-powerful men, a struggle between someone evil and someone good.

"I'll show you a mistake."

Ellen gazed in front her, looking up in time to see Ranger be swept off his feet by an invisible force and slammed into the wall of a nearby building. He slid down the stone bricks, and gathered a heap on the pathway. His body was limp and blood began to flow from his nose. He was lifeless.

Dead.

"Whoops. Sorry for that mistake," apologised Dvorak, oozing with sarcasm. And then he clapped briefly and stopped.

"Have you thought about joining me? You are obviously a man of many talents."

"Join you? Not if my life depended on it."

"Have it your way then," spat Lucien. "Get up," he sneered at Ellen, grabbing her with his free hand. He jerked her by the neck and made her kneel so that she was now facing Dvorak. Her legs started to ache again, the small rocks becoming sharper than ever. They bit at her skin painfully. The older man's eyes met hers and then flicked back to Lucien.

"Dvorak. Now who is laughing?" It was Lucien's turn to laugh now, the shrill noise painful to Ellen's ears. "Do you think you are in a position to say no? Do you?"

His hand gripped on her hair and pulled jerking her head backwards and exposing her neck.

"Two can play this game." The blade travelled around her neck now and then rested on a vein. "All it would take is a small slip and she would die."

Dvorak looked Lucien up and down, his eyes flicking back towards Ellen. He nodded at her – a movement so small it was almost invisible – and then folded his arms. His robes of black and silver were sodden and his hair was plastered downwards but he was still menacing and intimidating. "Oh, I wouldn't do that if I were you."

"And why not?" Lucien tugged on Ellen's hair even more. "I've got what you so desperately want."

"Because," Dvorak replied sharply. "The moment you move, you will die. Checkmate."

And his face broke into a wild, blood-hungry grin.

Chapter Twenty-Three

There was silence as Lucien recoiled his head, his eyes widening in surprise. Ellen watched as his hand was re-positioned near her neck, now applying more pressure on the blade. She sincerely hoped that Dvorak was not bluffing and even if something happened, he would be taken down with her.

Her pulse quickened.

"And why would that be?" he laughed.

But his laugh was nervous, almost knowing that the next few minutes would mean the difference between winning and losing; living and dying. The tables could turn and they could turn awfully quickly.

Dvorak remained standing in front of Lucien, tucking his arms behind his back. He said one word; one word which provided absolutely no reasoning: "Because."

Just as she was thinking – convincing– herself that it was a bluff, Ellen caught slaw movement from the top of her eyes. Someone had just stepped into view atop one of the museum turrets; someone whic h gave her hope and couldn't help but make her smile. He was a sight for her tired eyes and she was grateful that she was able to see him again.

His usually long, shimmering silver hair was tied up and his usual robes were changed for a black vest. He also wore a satchel but-

No, it wasn't a satchel. It was a quiver, the container poking out from behind his shoulder. His arms were outstretched, pulling back on an arrow which had been loaded. Was the game over for Lucien?

He let out a sigh of relief, an indication that he was expecting something much, much more; something more grand.

"You have but one person," he called out, loud enough for Hans to hear.

"You see. That's where you're wrong." Dvorak outstretched one his arms, a finger pointing into the distance.

He looked to where the man was pointing and swallowed hard. There was a split-second before he wrenched Ellen off the floor, her knees thanking for the reprieve. He pushed her to turn around so that she was now had the two figures on either side of her as if she was a human shield. She caught a glimpse of Claudia, dressed similarly to Hans, holding a daunting crossbow aimed directly at them.

"I'd re-evaluate the situation if I were you three," he yelled in desperation. He was clutching at straws now; straws that were disappearing as more of the situation unravelled. His ruthless, his tirades, appeared to be catching up with him. "All it takes is one stroke and she's gone. It would be a shame to lose such a beautiful girl but if it's needed, so be it!"

He ran a finger from Ellen's forehead, down her cheek and then stroked her neck. He kissed her forehead, the knife held steady.

I need you to move in front of him so I have a clean path, she heard Hans tell her.

If she moves, she dies. We only have one shot at this. The moment you move forward Ellen, Hans and I will need to shoot. It was Claudia this time, her commanding and strategic skills making a strong surge forward.

I'll do anything so long as we can get rid of him.

Ellen saw both of them retrain there weaponry, reapplying the tension to the projectiles. The strings on them were pulled tight as if it was a violin but this was no time to make music, and they weren't instruments. They were designed with one intent.

"So what will it be, you pieces of scum? Do I send her to Dvorak's children?" He shot a smile at Dvorak, the man still standing and trying to remain calm. There was no reply to Lucien's question, the silence driving him to be impatient. He took a deep breath, and shrugged.

"Have it your way then."

Ellen felt a burning sensation start at the side of her neck and she cried out in pain as it began to surge through her nerves. The rain washed at the open wound, stinging and washing away the blood which poured from it. The river stained her clothes, and formed a pool around her feet. And then it started carving a trail through the crevices in the bitumen and dripped into a nearby gutter.

She felt weak, lightheaded, but also infuriated like a rampaging bull. She struggled to remain standing however, she refused to back down from the fight. But then a heavy mass pushed onto her back, and it dragged her down to the road as it fell. Lucien's body fell on-top of her and she struggled to free herself from the man. Even in death, he clutched onto her. She let out a scream.

She heard hurried – running – footsteps approach her and a clank as Claudia put down her crossbow. Both Claudia and Dvorak leaned over her, Claudia's hands pushing onto Ellen's neck; Dvorak pulling Lucien off her.

"Don't move," he breathed to her as he heaved the weight off her. He dropped to his knees, and checked her pulse. It was still beating – it was still strong. "She will make it if we go now but she will need to be kept stable and off her feet. We will also need to go as quickly as we can. I clamped his communication but it's not a guarantee that he didn't have another method of contact."

There were more footsteps as Hans joined, sprinting to them from the turret. He placed his bow down, and held onto Ellen's hand.

"She'll be okay, yes?" he asked, staring at Dvorak. She could see his temples pulsing and hear the worry in his voice.

The old man shook his head in response. "If we move now. She's likely to make it, but we need better resources that are back at the manor. We need to pick her up and go."

Claudia picked up her crossbow, flinging it around her arm. "On the count of three then." Hans hastily picked up his bow, the bow which Ellen recognised to be hers. Hans had used her own weapon to kill the man that had entrapped her; tortured her.

"One. Two. Three."

Ellen felt herself being picked up, each of the three adults supporting a different part of her body. She cast a glance in Lucien's direction, relief washing over her that it was over.

That he was gone.

A bolt stuck out from his back, and an arrow protruded from his chest, piercing directly through his clothes. His eyes were closed and he was lying in a dam of blood. His hair was mottled, wet and red.

His own blood.

His own blood that was drawn to avenge all the innocent lives he had taken. Even the rain couldn't wash away his sins.

And now his own life was taken, like he used to take others; him never being able to take a single one again.

Justice had been brought.

She took a last look of Lucien's body and shed a tear, the fear and angst leaving her body.

And then she felt herself go weightless and the familiar darkness surrounded her.

Untouched.

Lightning Source UK Ltd.
Milton Keynes UK
UKHW020440211122
412554UK00016B/804